MURDER ON WOOF WAY

A WAGGING TAIL COZY MYSTERY

CINDY BELL

CONTENTS

Chapter 1	1
Chapter 2	13
Chapter 3	27
Chapter 4	39
Chapter 5	52
Chapter 6	61
Chapter 7	70
Chapter 8	83
Chapter 9	92
Chapter 10	102
Chapter 11	113
Chapter 12	123
Chapter 13	131
Chapter 14	139
Chapter 15	147
Chapter 16	155
Chapter 17	166
Chapter 18	174
Chapter 19	184
Chapter 20	194
Chapter 21	201
Chapter 22	208
About the Author	213
Also by Cindy Bell	215

Copyright © 2022 Cindy Bell

All rights reserved.

No part of this publication may be reproduced or transmitted in any form or by any means, electronic or mechanical, including photocopy, recording, or any information storage or retrieval system, without permission in writing from the publisher.

This is a work of fiction. The characters, incidents and locations portrayed in this book and the names herein are fictitious. Any similarity to or identification with the locations, names, characters or history of any person, product or entity is entirely coincidental and unintentional.

All trademarks and brands referred to in this book are for illustrative purposes only, are the property of their respective owners and not affiliated with this publication in any way. Any trademarks are being used without permission, and the publication of the trademark is not authorized by, associated with or sponsored by the trademark owner.

ISBN: 9798413610725

CHAPTER 1

"Settle down, drink your water." Nikki Green laughed as the three dogs at her feet fought over the water bowls she'd set down on the sidewalk. Dogs were welcome at her friend Gina's café outdoor seating area. In fact, Gina doted on them. She made sure they had special treats and plenty of water. That was one of the many reasons that Nikki loved to stop there on her morning walks with the dogs. And this morning she was even more excited to be there, because her boyfriend, Detective Quinn Grant, planned to meet her there. She untangled the leashes that belonged to Spots, Coco, and Sesame, then glanced up in time to see Quinn walking toward her. Instantly, her heart pounded faster.

"I see you brought the kids." Quinn settled in a chair at the small table outside.

"They're all so excited to see you." Nikki grinned as Spots and Coco fought to lick Quinn's hands.

"Don't you get enough of me at home, Spots?" Quinn laughed and stroked the top of the Dalmatian's head. Then he reached his hand out in an attempt to pet Sesame.

The tiny dog gave a sharp growl.

"Yikes!" Quinn snatched his hand back. "She's not too friendly, huh?"

"She is a bit opinionated." Nikki grinned as she stroked her fingers through the Toy Poodle's curly hair.

"Apparently, she doesn't have a very high opinion of me." Quinn met Nikki's eyes as he looked up from the dog. "I hope it doesn't spread."

"Oh stop, she's just nervous around new people." Nikki looked back into his eyes. "Trust me, my opinion couldn't be any higher of you."

"You're just saying that to make me feel better, aren't you?"

"I'm saying it because I mean it." Nikki smiled. "Quinn, our time together has been great."

"It has, hasn't it?" Quinn nodded. "If only I'd

known back in high school, what I know now, maybe I wouldn't have waited so long to figure that out."

"You knew enough to rescue me from drowning." Nikki laughed. "Of course, I had no idea that you'd run off and join the police force."

"And I had no idea that you'd run off with my heart." Quinn quirked an eyebrow, then grinned. "Too cheesy?"

"Maybe just a little." Nikki draped her hand over his.

"Coffee?" Gina stepped out of the café with a coffee pot in one hand and two mugs in the other.

"Yes, please." Nikki looked over at her.

"Thank you." Quinn nodded to Gina, then pulled his cell phone out of his pocket. He gazed at the screen for a moment, then typed out a quick message.

"Work?" Nikki watched tension etch its way across Quinn's boyish features.

"Yes, but I still have a few more minutes." Quinn glanced up at Gina as she poured coffee into his mug. "Thanks so much. I've been looking forward to this all morning. You make the best coffee."

"Well, you know I grow and gather the beans

myself." Gina winked as she took a step back from the table.

"Sure you do." Nikki grinned as she met her friend's eyes. "I guess you must get up pretty early in the morning."

"Early enough to see you out with your pups." Gina crouched down to pet the dogs curled up by Nikki's chair. "Aren't you just the cutest, most precious, most adorable, little things." She stroked her hand over Sesame's head.

"What, no growls for her?" Quinn crossed his arms. "I'm going to start taking this personally."

"Her owner is a woman, so she's probably more comfortable around women." Nikki shrugged, then bit into her bottom lip to hide a smile at the faint pout on Quinn's lips. "Don't worry, Spots still loves you."

"I sure hope so." Quinn held out his hand to Spots, who promptly licked it.

"See?" Nikki glanced down the sidewalk in both directions, then looked back at Gina as she straightened up. "I haven't seen Walter and his pup lately. Usually, he's here at the same time we are."

"Oh, there's a bit of a scandal going on about that." Gina glanced over her shoulder at the sound of her name being called from inside the café. "I'm sorry, I have to go."

"Wait, what about Walter?" Nikki called out.

"I'll have to fill you in later." Gina disappeared inside the café.

"I actually have to go, too." Quinn took a big swallow of his coffee, then slid the mug across the table to her. "Finish that up for me, will you?"

"Sure." Nikki nodded. "I hope it's nothing too serious."

"Just a dispute between neighbors." Quinn rolled his eyes. "The usual petty stuff." He stood up and leaned across the table to kiss her.

Nikki smiled through the kiss.

Quinn crouched down to say goodbye to the dogs. As he reached out to pet Spots and Coco, Sesame snarled at him. "Okay, okay." He shook his head as he looked at the little dog. "I've been told that I'm quite likable, you know?"

"You are."

As Nikki watched him walk away, she thought about how her life had turned out. Things had not gone as planned so far in her life. At twenty-four she had expected to be quite a bit further along. Instead, she still lived in her small apartment, and walked the same dogs she'd been walking for a few years, along with a few new ones. She yearned to have the rescue she dreamed of, a large property, big enough to house plenty of animals and give them the kind of life they deserved to have. But it seemed as distant as ever.

"Pancakes." Gina brought out two plates. "Oh no, where did Quinn go?"

"He had to run. Work." Nikki looked at the pancakes. "I didn't order these."

"No, they're on the house. You have to try them." Gina sat down across from her. "I guess I'll just have to join you, then."

"That would be wonderful." As Nikki looked at the pancakes she realized how hungry she was. She hadn't had time for breakfast that morning. She picked up her fork and took a bite of the pancakes. "Oh, wow! These are amazing!"

"Aren't they?" Gina's eyes widened. "The best I've ever tasted."

"Your pancakes are always great, but these are out of this world. Is the cook doing something different?" Nikki took another bite.

"Actually, it's a new cook. Hang on, I want you to meet him." Gina walked back into the café just as Quinn walked back up to the table.

"Back so soon?" Nikki smiled. "Did you lock everyone up?"

"Not just yet." Quinn laughed as he snatched his keys up from where he'd left them on the table. "Can't exactly be a good detective, if you can't remember to take your keys with you when you leave."

"Here, you have to try these." Nikki cut off a piece of her pancake, scooped it up with her fork, and held it out to him. "Come on, have a bite."

"I really have to go." Quinn frowned.

"You have time for one bite." Nikki pushed the pancake closer to his mouth.

"Alright." Quinn sighed and opened his mouth. The moment the pancake slid off of the fork, his eyes widened. "Wow! These are great!"

"Thanks." A deep and unfamiliar voice drew Nikki's attention to the man who had walked up beside Gina. He appeared to be in his early thirties, with a thick mop of brown curls, and rich brown eyes. His gaze locked to Nikki's instantly. "I'm glad you like them."

"Nikki, Quinn, this is Alex." Gina patted his thick arm. "He's the best thing that has ever happened to my café."

"It's good to meet you." Quinn offered his hand. "Those pancakes are great."

"Thanks." Alex took his hand in a firm shake. As he did, his sleeve slid up along his elbow and revealed more of his upper arm.

Quinn's eyes settled on a tattoo that peeked out from under Alex's sleeve. He pulled his hand away, then looked over at Nikki.

"Why don't you get those pancakes to go?"

"To go? Why? I have time." Nikki looked back at Alex. "You have to tell me what the secret ingredient in these pancakes is."

"I would." Alex leaned one hand against the table as he looked into her eyes. "But then, I'd have to kill you."

Nikki laughed but noticed that Quinn's jaw rippled with tension.

"I'd better get back to work. It was nice meeting you folks." Alex nodded to all three of them, then walked back into the café.

"Did you do any research on this guy before you hired him?" Quinn looked over at Gina, his eyes narrowed.

"I did enough." Gina crossed her arms.

Nikki stared at Quinn. He didn't often look

angry, but he certainly did at the moment. "Do you know him, Quinn?"

"No, I don't know him. I don't have to know him, to recognize that tattoo on his arm. It means he's done time in maximum security prison." Quinn frowned as he glanced at her, then looked back at Gina. "You should run background checks on your employees."

"I know about his checkered past." Gina stared into his eyes. "I believe in giving people second chances."

"For him to be in that prison, he had to commit a pretty serious crime, Gina. You, employing him here just encourages him to stay in our town, potentially putting everyone in danger." Quinn shook his head.

"I think that's judging someone unfairly, Quinn." Gina glared at him, then clucked her tongue. "Nikki, you and the pups are always welcome here but you might want to work on opening your boyfriend's mind a little."

"I don't know what's going on here, but let's not judge too hastily." Nikki stood up to try and defuse the situation. "I'm sure that if Gina hired him, it's because she believes that he's a good person."

"I do." Gina nodded. "Whatever crime he committed, he's done the time for it. Doesn't that give him the right to live out the rest of his life in peace?"

"I just think you need to be cautious. You can hire anyone you want of course but just be careful." Quinn held up his hands as his cell phone buzzed. "I have to go." He turned and rushed back toward his car.

"Wow, he was quick to judge." Gina watched him go.

"He isn't usually." Nikki frowned. "Gina, are you sure about this guy you hired?"

"I am." Gina turned her attention to Nikki. "I believe in giving people second chances in life."

"So do I." Nikki sat back down and picked up her fork. "Now, I'm going to finish these pancakes."

"Enjoy." Gina tipped her head toward Nikki's mug. "I'll bring you a refill."

"Thanks." Nikki heard Quinn's car pull away. She couldn't help but wonder why he'd had such a strong reaction to Alex's presence. She knew that he saw a lot more as a detective than she could ever imagine. He'd worked many serious cases. He'd also been involved in the prisons from time to time. Sure, his behavior that morning surprised her, but she wondered what he'd experienced that made him rush to judgment like that. Maybe he was just being overprotective.

As Nikki had a bite of pancake she looked down at the dogs. They were all lying near her feet having a sleep. She laughed as she noticed that Spots had cuddled right up to Coco. They had certainly become good friends and she loved seeing them together. However, she knew the dogs wouldn't be relaxed for much longer, so she ate quickly. As she finished her food, Coco stirred and started to sit up.

"Good timing, buddy." Nikki patted his head as she gathered up the dogs' leashes and left an ample tip on the table. She didn't want Gina to have any hard feelings against Quinn, but she realized it might be too late for that. "Alright, let's walk off those pancakes." She laughed.

Naturally slim, if not a little too skinny, her size did not indicate her appetite. She enjoyed a big meal, but she also spent so much time walking and often running with the dogs that she burnt it off quickly.

As the dogs led her in the direction of the park, nicknamed Pooch Park by the locals because it was popular for dogs, Sesame began to bark as she spotted a squirrel headed for a nearby tree.

"Settle down, girl, that squirrel is practically

bigger than you." Nikki laughed. After dropping Spots off at Quinn's house and Coco at his house, she took Sesame for another walk through the park, then led the dog across the street to the section of town filled with large houses and larger properties. She headed for one home in particular. She noticed a pile of boxes inside the open door of the two-car garage. Labels were scrawled on the side with black marker. Kitchen, bathroom, basement.

"I guess Mom is still getting settled in, huh?" Nikki smiled down at Sesame as the tiny dog led her up the winding driveway to the wide, stone porch. When they reached the front door, Nikki did her best to keep Sesame from scratching at the door. She knocked lightly, then took a step back as she waited for Julie to answer.

The door swung open and a petite woman in her fifties stepped out through it. "Where have you been?" Her tiny nose scrunched up as she looked at Nikki.

CHAPTER 2

"Am I late?" Nikki raised an eyebrow, then checked her watch. It appeared she was right on time give or take a few minutes.

"No, you're not late, but I would like to know where you took my Sesame." Julie scooped up the tiny dog and tugged her leash free of Nikki's grasp.

"Oh, we went on our walk, then we stopped by Gina's café for a drink and a treat, then we walked back here through the park." Nikki smiled as she pulled out her phone. "I took a few photographs because I thought you might like to see them."

"No, thank you. I never gave you permission to take her to the café, did I?" Julie patted the top of the dog's head. "I hired you to take her for a walk. I never said that you could get a coffee on the way."

"I outlined our possible outings in the paperwork that you signed when you hired me." Nikki did her best to keep her tone calm. "Of course, if there are places you would prefer I not walk Sesame, or if you'd rather I walk her alone, I can make those arrangements."

"I just don't want you taking Sesame to that café." Julie huffed as she shifted Sesame from one arm to the other. "It's important to me that Sesame be socialized, so that she can interact with other dogs, and people. Her therapist says it's important. But I do not want her going to that café."

"Yes, I did notice that she had some trouble with men." Nikki offered her hand to Sesame, who licked it. "Is there a particular reason that you didn't want her going to Gina's café?" She tried to meet Julie's eyes.

"I'd rather not discuss it. Please, don't take her anywhere near that place again. Understand?" Julie looked back at Nikki, her eyes sharp.

"Yes, I understand. I'm sorry if I've upset you. I'll be sure to respect your wishes from now on." Nikki held back her desire to point out that Julie had never actually told her not to take Sesame to the café. When it came to owning a business, Nikki had learned that it was best to let the customer always be right and apologize as often as possible. She might not like all of the owners of the dogs she walked, but without them, she wouldn't be able to do what she loved and she wouldn't be able to pay her rent.

"I'll see you this afternoon for Sesame's walk." Nikki smiled.

"Actually, she won't need one this afternoon. I'm taking her on a special day out." Julie made kissing noises at the dog.

Sesame wagged her tail and jumped at Julie's face with a frenzy of licks.

"I hope you both have fun." Nikki's heart warmed at the dog's excitement. "I'll see you tomorrow morning, then?"

"Yes, tomorrow." Julie stepped into the house and closed the door.

Nikki lingered there for a moment. She wondered why Julie didn't want her taking Sesame to Gina's. Her curiosity started to go into overdrive. With all of Julie's wealth, was it possible that she just didn't want her dog seen at a little café? Wasn't it up to her standards? Or was there a more personal reason why she didn't want her dog going to that particular café?

"Stop it, Nikki," she muttered to herself as she

walked back down the driveway to the sidewalk. "There's a difference between curiosity and nosiness." She'd been trying to get better about not questioning everything about everyone she met. It wasn't so much about lack of trust as it was about wanting to know the truth. Some people tended to present a very different image from who they really were, and she preferred to get to know the real person.

As Nikki walked in the direction of her friend, Sonia Whitter's, house, she felt her excitement grow some. She looked forward to seeing Sonia, and her dog, Princess, every day. Sonia loved dogs and she was very protective of Princess. Often Nikki would walk Princess alone, so that the Chihuahua got a break from the larger dogs, and so that she and Sonia could walk together. It was only relatively recently that Sonia allowed Princess to walk with other dogs. Plus it gave Nikki and Sonia time to talk without having to monitor ten different noses pulling in ten different directions.

As Nikki passed an older, single-story house she heard sharp words float through an open window.

"I don't care what the licensing board says, I want my complaint filed, and I want an inspector out there tomorrow. What kind of town allows businesses to run wild like this?"

The man's voice sounded familiar to Nikki but she couldn't place it. She jumped at the sound of a crash. He shouted even louder.

"Just get it done."

Nikki guessed that in his fit of anger he'd broken something in the house. She quickened her pace. As much as she wanted to find out who the voice belonged to, his anger had her on edge and she was running late.

Nikki tried to put the memory of his temper out of her mind as she passed a section of newer, towering, three-story houses that the locals called eyesores and atrocities, to reach Sonia's house. Though her property was large, as was her house, it was a more classic style.

Sonia stepped out the door as Nikki approached, with Princess at her heels. "Nikki, Princess has been waiting by the door." Sonia laughed.

"Sorry, I got held up for a few minutes when I dropped off Sesame." Nikki smiled as she stepped up onto the porch with Sonia and Princess. "Hi, baby." She crouched down to greet Princess. The Chihuahua wagged her tail as Nikki patted her.

"Oh, Julie." Sonia rolled her eyes. "I can only imagine the run-around she gives you. All she ever talks about is Sesame and all of the competitions that little dog has won. Sure, she's cute, but there's more to life than dog competitions." She reached down and gave Princess a few strokes on her back as Nikki stood up. "Isn't that right, Princess?"

Princess jumped up on Nikki's leg and gave a sharp bark.

"Oh, impatient are we?" Nikki grinned. "I've been looking forward to our walk, too."

"I'm so glad to see you." Sonia hugged her, then took a step back and narrowed her eyes. "What's wrong?"

"Huh? Nothing." Nikki crouched down again and scratched behind Princess' ear.

"You look distracted." Sonia frowned as she looked down at her friend. "I can tell something is bothering you."

"How can you tell?" Nikki looked up at her with wide eyes. "Does it show somehow?"

"Not exactly. It's just that most of the time, especially when you're with the dogs, you look pretty relaxed. But right now, you might be smiling, but I can still see the tension in your face." Sonia tipped her head back and forth. "I know that may seem a little strange, but I can't help it, Nikki. I worry about you, you know."

"You shouldn't." Nikki straightened up and looked into her eyes. She was shocked that Sonia knew her so well, that she could tell that something was bothering her. The truth was she couldn't get Quinn's reaction to Alex out of her mind, but she didn't want to discuss it, at least not yet. She just wanted to try to put the thought out of her head. "I promise, I'm just fine."

"Just fine?" Sonia continued to stare back at her.

"I'm just distracted." Nikki shrugged.

"Okay." Sonia nodded knowingly. "Well, if you want to talk about it, let me know."

"Thanks, Sonia."

"Now, let's get started on our walk, so you can start to relax." Sonia gestured down the street.

"Good idea. Things always seem to make more sense when I'm in motion." Nikki started down the sidewalk.

"Princess looks so happy." Sonia looked at the eager dog walking along the street.

"Yes, and she's loving her walks with the other

dogs as well." Nikki grinned. "That is as long as they let her take the lead, she's happy."

"Absolutely." Sonia laughed as they continued around the block. They stopped for Princess as she sniffed a flower. "That's about it for me." She stretched her arms above her head, then rubbed a hand along her hip. "I'll walk more tomorrow, but I think I pulled a muscle at my Tai Chi class."

"Are you okay?" Nikki frowned as she gazed at her friend. "Do you want me to walk with you back to the house?"

"No, you two go ahead. Princess loves having her walks with you. I'll be fine getting back." Sonia waved her hand. "And don't forget, just because I'm older than you, that doesn't mean I'm not as spry."

"I won't forget." Nikki grinned. The nearly fifty year age difference between her and Sonia didn't impact their friendship much but there were times when Nikki could get a little too overprotective of her. She didn't like the thought of her friend being hurt, or overly burdened. Was that part of the reason for Quinn's reaction earlier in the day? Maybe there was something about Alex that he considered to be dangerous and he wanted to protect Nikki and Gina. He'd mentioned Alex's possible crimes, but she knew that Quinn didn't often rush to judgment, so what about Alex had made him react that way?

Nikki decided to skip the park and head back to the café. She wanted to find out a little bit more about Alex, and why Walter had stopped visiting the café.

About a block from the café, Princess stopped to sniff a tree. As Nikki waited for her, she noticed a car rolling slowly along the road. The car continued to inch by. She looked into the window of the driver's side and saw a man and a woman. They were dressed in business suits. Were they looking at Princess? The small, sweet dog often drew looks of admiration from people.

As Nikki continued toward the café, the car appeared to match her pace. She paused as she reached the outside tables and watched as the car continued to roll by. If it had been following her, it appeared that the driver was no longer interested in what she was up to. Or maybe they didn't want to look too suspicious. Nikki shrugged it off.

"Maybe they're just scoping out the town," Nikki murmured to Princess as she picked her up in her arms. She waved through the front window at Gina. She'd already put up her closed sign for the day, as she closed early on Mondays. She only served breakfast.

Gina pushed open the door and waved to her.

"Be right out, I'm just closing up."

"We'll be right here." Nikki settled at one of the tables and gave Princess enough leeway on her leash to allow her to explore without getting too close to the road.

When Gina stepped out through the front door again she had a bowl of water in one hand and a special homemade dog biscuit in the shape of a bone in the other. She grinned as Princess ran right up to her.

"Hi, baby. Here you go." She offered her the treat, then set the bowl of water down by the table.

"I'm so sorry about the way Quinn talked to you this morning. He seemed to overreact when he saw Alex's tattoo." Nikki frowned as her friend sat down across from her. "I can't get it off of my mind."

"Trust me, he isn't the first person who has had a problem with Alex. That's why Walter wasn't here today." Gina sighed as she sat back in the chair. "It's not like I don't understand the concerns that come with hiring a reformed criminal, but if I don't hire him, who will? He's done his time, he wants to put his life back together, but how can he do that without a job to support him?"

"You're doing a good thing, Gina." Nikki met her eyes. "I get it."

"He strikes me as a good guy." Gina leaned forward to look at Nikki. "He went to high school with my cousin, and he just ended up involved with the wrong crowd. What happened is terrible, of course, but it's in the past. I just wanted to give him a chance to do something good with his life, something better than he's been able to do. Sure, being a cook isn't going to change his world, but it's a stepping-stone back to a normal life for him."

"I think it's a great thing you're doing." Nikki looked into her eyes. "I can also understand why Quinn was concerned. But I'll talk to him. What about Walter? What happened with him?"

"When he saw Alex, he threw a fit. He told me I couldn't employ him here. He was so angry." Gina's eyes widened. "Walter has always been kind and a great tipper, but I can't put up with that kind of behavior in my café. He can't tell me who I can and cannot employ. I asked him not to come back. Luckily, so far, he hasn't."

"I'm sorry, Gina, you're only trying to do

something good, and you keep getting a hard time for it."

"It's okay. I knew I'd catch some flak for hiring him. I just feel bad for Alex. He told me he feels so guilty for all of the trouble. I keep trying to explain to him that it's not his fault. But he doesn't want to listen. I'm afraid he might quit."

"That would be a shame." Nikki frowned as she stood up from the table. "I'd better get Princess back home. Good luck with Alex. I hope he decides to stay."

"I hope so, too." Gina headed back into the café.

Nikki led Princess down the sidewalk, but as she neared the corner to cross the street, Princess began to growl.

"What's wrong?" Nikki peered down at the dog.

Princess crouched down against the sidewalk and growled again.

Nikki followed her line of sight and saw Woof Way, the alley beside the café.

"What is it, a raccoon?" Nikki grinned as she scooped Princess up into her arms. "Don't worry, you can leave him alone, I won't let him hurt you."

Princess nestled against her chest but continued to growl.

Curiosity burned through Nikki's mind. Sure,

it's probably just a raccoon, but Princess had seen plenty of those and never acted like this, she usually just wanted to chase them. For being a small dog, she was quite bold, and often bossed around the bigger dogs, but she had rarely heard her growl.

"Let's have a look." Nikki started down Woof Way.

A sudden shriek made her gasp and jump back.

"Gina?" She spotted her friend at the other end of the alley, where the side door that led to the back of the café opened up onto it. She had her back to Nikki, but another scream made it clear that something was very wrong.

"Gina!"

Nikki hurried down the alley in the direction of her screaming friend, with Princess held tight against her chest. As she drew closer she could clearly see that Gina trembled from head to toe. She stumbled backward and bumped right into Nikki and Princess.

"Oh! Don't hurt me, please!" Gina gasped as she put her hands up to shield her face.

"Gina, it's okay, it's me." Nikki wrapped her free arm around her and pulled her close as she surveyed the alley for any threat. "It's okay, you're safe." She looked past her friend toward a pool of blood on the pavement in front of her.

Shocked, Nikki stared at the drops of blood that formed a trail that ran toward the dumpster. Lying beside it was a body, his arm splayed out to the side. Nikki recognized the tattoo that Quinn had noticed earlier.

CHAPTER 3

"Alex?" Nikki's heart raced. "Is that Alex? What happened, Gina?"

"I don't know." Gina clung tightly to Nikki. "I just found him like this. I think someone shot him." She looked at her with tear-filled eyes. "Nikki, who could do something like this?"

"I'm so sorry, Gina." Nikki hugged her again as she heard sirens wail in the distance. "Did you call for help?"

"I think so." Gina pointed at her phone on the ground, right by Alex's body. "I went over to try to help him and I was so scared, I dropped it, and then I couldn't pick it up again, I just couldn't. It was so close to him."

"It's alright." Nikki patted Princess as she

squirmed in her arms. "Everything is going to be alright."

"How?" Gina shook her head. "I told him he would have a second chance here, Nikki. I told him he could change his life. I told him this was a new beginning."

"None of this is your fault, Gina." Nikki smoothed her hand down through her friend's hair. "Just try to breathe. It's quite a shock, I know, but everything is going to be okay."

"I just don't understand." Gina shook her head. "I was talking to him right before I came out to talk with you. How could this happen? How could I not have known that someone killed him?"

"Why didn't we see or hear anything?" Nikki narrowed her eyes as she gazed toward the body. The alley wasn't far from where she and Gina had been talking.

The sirens grew louder just before several police cars skidded to a stop at the end of the alley. A few officers surged forward, but Nikki only focused on the man in a suit who jogged toward her.

"Quinn!" Nikki called out to him as Gina pulled away from her. "Something terrible has happened."

"Are you okay?" Quinn looked from Nikki to Gina. "Are either of you hurt?"

"No. We're not hurt." Gina pointed a trembling finger at the body. "But Alex is."

Quinn ran forward and peered around the side of the dumpster. He immediately began barking orders at the other officers that arrived at the scene.

Nikki's mind spun with all of the activity that was unfolding around her. Despite her dizziness, she focused in on Gina. If she was this overwhelmed, she guessed that Gina had to be even more lost. It wasn't exactly the first dead body that Nikki had seen.

"Let's get you out front." Nikki took her by the arm and steered her toward the end of the alley. "We have to let the police do their work now, and we need to get you sitting down."

"Yes, I should sit down." Gina nodded.

Nikki guided her to the front of the café and pulled out a chair for her. She helped her settle, then looked up to see Sonia right in front of her.

"Nikki, what's happening?" Sonia took Princess out of Nikki's arms and cuddled her close. She licked Sonia's cheek. "Are you okay? My neighbor told me something was happening at the café. Then I wasn't able to reach you. I had to see if you were both okay."

"How could this happen?" Gina shook her head.

"Nikki, tell me what's going on." Sonia locked her eyes to Nikki's. "Is someone hurt?"

"One of Gina's employees, the new cook." Nikki looked up at Sonia. "He's dead."

"Not Alex?" Sonia's eyes widened. "That young man that just started a week or two ago?"

"Yes, Alex." Nikki frowned as she studied Sonia. "Did you know him well?"

"It's Alex, poor Alex!" Gina cupped her hand over her mouth and began to sob again.

"She needs some tea, I'll get us some tea." Sonia walked past both of them and into the café.

Nikki pulled her chair up beside Gina's and spoke to her softly.

"Just focus on breathing right now, Gina. All of this is too much to take in, I know that. Right now, all you need to think about is breathing." She took a slow breath as she placed her hand over Gina's. "In, and out." She breathed out and gave her friend's hand a gentle squeeze.

"In, and out." Gina nodded as she did her best to mimic Nikki's actions. Tears continued to slide down her cheeks.

As Nikki studied the pain in her expression, she wondered whether there might have been another reason that Gina decided to give Alex a second chance. She recalled how happy she seemed to be around Alex. Had Gina and Alex been in a relationship? Alex was at least ten years younger than Gina. Nikki couldn't picture them being in a relationship but it was still possible. She bit into her bottom lip and tried to think of a subtle way to ask the question.

"Gina?" Nikki looked into her eyes. "You and Alex were pretty close, weren't you?"

"I didn't know him well." Gina took another deep breath, then blew it out slowly.

"But you had a connection?" Nikki scooted closer to her.

"Nikki!" Quinn's voice called from the entrance of the alley.

"Yes?" Nikki stood up and started to walk toward him.

"I'm going to need a statement, stick around, okay?" Quinn met her eyes.

"I will." Nikki held his gaze for a moment. She could see the tension in his face. As she turned back to Gina, she hoped that her hunch was wrong. She hoped that Gina and Alex didn't have any kind of romantic relationship. She didn't want her to have lost someone very close to her.

"Gina, were you and Alex together?" Nikki

blurted out the question as she sat back down beside her.

"No." Gina looked over at her. "No, of course not."

Sonia held Princess in her arms as the café door closed behind her. She looked over the area as she rushed toward the kitchen. Chairs had already been stacked on top of the tables. A strong smell of cleaner indicated that the floors had recently been mopped. She could see that the counters shined as if they had just been wiped down.

"Come on, Princess, we need to be quick."

Princess looked at her and barked once as if she agreed with her.

Sonia opened the kitchen door, expecting the police to be there, but when no one was she rushed over to the sink. She wanted to get Gina some tea to calm her nerves and she knew she only had a few minutes to see if there was anything in the kitchen that could be a clue as to who killed Alex. If the police found her inside, they would kick her out straight away.

Sonia decided to heat the water in the

microwave. It wasn't ideal but it was quick. She held Princess in one arm as she busied herself grabbing two cups and filling them with water. As she did, she searched the kitchen for any sign that something was out of place. It was likely that Alex had spent his last minutes in this very space. Had he left any clues about who his killer was?

Princess eagerly sniffed the air as the smells were new to her.

"Helping me sniff out the clues, aren't you, baby?" Sonia whispered to Princess as she kissed the top of her head.

Sonia continued to look around the kitchen. She noticed a pad of paper by the phone. As she walked over to the microwave, she took out her phone and snapped a picture of the paper. It looked like a phone number. On the other side of the room she saw a long pole propped up against the wall. It didn't look like any kitchen tool she'd ever seen before. One side was taped, as if to serve as a grip for the person wielding it.

With its nearness to the door, she wondered if it might have been positioned there to use for self-defense. She snapped a picture of it, just as the microwave beeped. Princess looked toward it as a deep voice called from the other side of the kitchen door. "Who's in there?"

Sonia gasped as she clutched Princess close. "The police are outside!" She hoped that a warning might cause whoever it was to take off.

"No, the police are inside." The kitchen door swung open and an officer stepped through it. "Who let you come in here?"

"Uh, no one let me." Sonia cleared her throat. "I just thought I'd make some tea for my friends outside."

"This building is part of a crime scene." The officer squinted at her. "Were you not aware of that?"

"I guess, I didn't really think about it. There wasn't any police tape up." Sonia pursed her lips. "The crime took place outside, didn't it?"

"That's what we're trying to figure out." The officer frowned. "They are putting the tape up now."

As the officer walked toward Sonia, she suddenly recognized him.

"Johnny? Johnny Parkers?"

"Yes." The officer squinted.

"I'm Sonia Whitter, I play cards with your mother, Doris, I have for years." Sonia smiled as she patted his cheek with her free hand. "I haven't seen you in ages."

"Sorry, I didn't recognize you, Mrs. Whitter." The officer pointed to the door. "Please, I need you to leave, before you contaminate the crime scene."

Sonia smiled at him as she stroked Princess' fur. Princess leaned forward, trying to get to the officer.

"Sorry, I didn't mean to do anything wrong. It's just that my nerves are frazzled by all of this, and I'm sure that Gina's are, too. I thought a cup of tea can go a long way to relaxing the mind. If the mind is relaxed, then Gina might be able to remember something that can help you solve this terrible crime. Don't you think?"

"Probably." The officer nodded.

"Okay, I'll go give her the tea, it's almost ready. Maybe if you could just hold Princess for me, I can carry out the cups." Sonia passed Princess over to him in the same moment that she pushed past him and quickly finished making the tea. "Thank you. Aw, look how much she likes you." She grabbed the cups and smiled as Princess licked the side of the officer's face.

"She is a cutie." The officer grinned as he endured the licks.

"Do you have any idea what happened to the man in the alley?" Sonia looked over at him.

"At this point we are still gathering evidence." The officer frowned.

"I understand that." Sonia nodded. "But I'm sure that you at least know how he was killed. Right?" She turned to face him with one cup in each hand.

"I guess." The officer looked into her eyes. "I doubt that my boss would want me to tell you about it."

"It's not like I'm not going to hear about it. You know how this town talks." Sonia shrugged. "You might as well tell me before I get mixed-up information from rumors."

"He was shot." The officer cleared his throat.

"Shot?" Sonia took a sharp breath. "How terrible. Did they find the gun?" She raised an eyebrow. "Was there a silencer?"

"We don't know yet." The officer sighed, then pushed the door of the kitchen open. "You better get out of here."

"Okay." Sonia nodded and offered a polite smile as she stepped past him into the front of the café. "So, you didn't find the murder weapon then?"

"I'm not saying another word. I've already said too much." The officer gestured toward the front of the café with his free hand. They walked into the dining area.

"Oops, oh dear, I'm sorry, could you just hold these for a moment." Sonia held out the cups to him. "I just heard my earring hit the floor. Please, just let me take a quick look around for it. Please?" She looked into his eyes.

"Fine!" The officer hooked his fingers through both handles of the cups so quickly that a bit of hot liquid splashed on his hands. "Ouch!"

"Oh dear, oh no, that won't do." Sonia reached for a napkin holder on one of the tables.

"No! Don't touch anything!" The officer narrowed his eyes. "Just find your earring, and quickly."

"Do be careful with my Princess, she is such a delicate creature." Sonia smiled at him.

Princess licked his cheek again.

The officer sighed and looked up at the ceiling as he managed to hold the little dog with one hand and balance the two hot cups in the other.

Sonia did her best not to give away the truth as she began to search around on the floor. It wasn't that easy to get on her knees, but once down there, she slipped her phone out of her pocket, and began to take a video of the surrounding café. Everywhere she supposedly looked for her earring, she did her best to get a recording of the café. Once she tucked her phone back into her pocket, she straightened up and looked at the officer.

"Oh, silly me, it was in my ear the whole time." Sonia laughed, then shook her head. "I guess I was just hearing things."

"Wow. Unbelievable." Officer Parkers glared at her, then tipped his head toward the door. "Let's go, outside."

"Okay, I'm going, I'm going." Sonia took the cups from him and stepped through the door as he held it open for her.

Princess jumped down out of his arms and bolted straight toward Nikki.

CHAPTER 4

Sonia held her breath as she followed Princess toward Nikki and Gina with the cups in her hands. From the look on Nikki's face she could tell that things weren't going well.

"Here." Sonia handed them each a cup of tea. "Drink some."

"How could this happen?" Gina clutched the cup between her palms.

Nikki blew across the top of her tea. She had no answer for her friend. She had no idea how someone could be killed in the alley, mere feet from where they chatted, without them seeing or hearing a thing. But she wanted to find out.

"Ladies." Quinn walked up to them and offered a quick nod. His eyes lingered on Sonia for a moment, before he turned his attention to Gina. "I know that this is a very difficult time, but I do have a few questions that I need to ask."

"Anything I can do." Gina nodded. "I just want to know what happened to Alex."

"That's what I'm here to find out." Quinn leaned his hands against the table as he looked at Gina. "Exactly how long was it between the last time you saw Alex, and when you found him in the alley?" He pulled out his tablet, prepared to type his notes on it.

"Maybe like, ten or fifteen minutes?" Gina looked across the table at Nikki. "I can't remember exactly. How long were we talking?"

"I'm not sure, but it couldn't have been much longer than that." Nikki frowned.

"So, he was alone in the café for about fifteen minutes?" Quinn made a note on his tablet. "Was anyone else inside the café?"

"We had already closed for the day." Gina shook her head. "I only serve breakfast on Mondays. Tyler, the busboy, had already left for the day." She took a shaky breath. "No one else was in there. Alex was alone." She frowned. "At least until he went into the alley."

"Why would he have been in the alley?" Quinn asked.

"He was probably taking the trash out." Gina looked up at him. "He always took it out a bit after closing."

"What about any customers?" Quinn narrowed his eyes as he studied her. "Maybe someone was still in the bathroom? Or had hidden somewhere inside the café?"

"I usually do a run through of the café before I lock the doors. I check the bathroom. I mean, I just stick my head in and call out to make sure no one is there, but there isn't a lot of space in there for someone to hide." Gina sat back in her chair and closed her eyes.

"And today, did you check the bathroom as usual?" Quinn cleared his throat. "It's really important to let me know if you did or not."

"I think I did." Gina opened her eyes, then winced. "I'm sorry, it's like everything is this huge mess in my head, and I can't figure out what I did today or the day before."

"It's okay." Nikki put her hand over Gina's in an attempt to soothe her. "It's normal to feel overwhelmed and confused by something like this. Just try to take a few deep breaths."

"And have some tea, too." Sonia nodded and edged the cup closer to Gina. "It will help."

"Thank you, but I don't want any tea." Gina stood up from her chair. "I want Alex not to be dead! I want this whole day to start over and things to go far differently! I don't know if there was someone in the bathroom, I can't remember if I checked it. I don't know if anyone was hiding in the café. I never once considered that there might be a murderer waiting to pop up at any moment!"

"Of course you didn't." Nikki stood up.

"I don't want you to solve Alex's murder." Gina ignored Nikki and looked at Quinn as she backed away from the table. "I saw the way you looked at him this morning. You didn't care about him then, and you're not going to care about him now! I want a different detective on the case."

"Gina." Nikki's heart pounded as she reached for her friend's hand. "Please, he's here to help, I promise. Quinn is great at his job. You know that."

"Gina, I can assure you that I will do everything in my power to find his murderer." Quinn straightened up and took a step away from the table. "I'll give you some time."

Nikki noticed that his movements were deliberate, as if he thought each one through before executing it. She read the tension in his expression, and the way he moved. "I can stay with her."

"Good." Quinn met Nikki's eyes briefly, then walked back over to the group of officers near the end of the alley.

"You don't have to stay." Gina sank back down in her chair. "I just want all of this to be over."

"I understand." Nikki rubbed her hand across Gina's shoulders. "Maybe we should get you home."

"Not with those clothes." An officer stepped up beside Nikki. "I'm afraid we're going to need them."

"My clothes?" Gina's eyes widened. "But why?"

"Because there might be evidence on them from when you checked Alex." The officer shrugged.

"Do you have a change of clothes here?" Nikki looked into Gina's eyes, which flitted nervously from Nikki to the officer, and back to Nikki again.

"Huh?" Gina blinked.

"Clothes? Do you have another shirt somewhere?" Nikki continued to hold her gaze.

"Oh yes, yes. I have a change of clothes. Sometimes it's like I live here. They're just in the office." Gina stood up and started toward the door.

"I'll go with you." The officer started to follow her.

"No, let me." Nikki stepped in front of him.

"That's not what I was instructed to do." The officer narrowed his eyes as he looked at Nikki.

"Officer Packer, right?"

"Parkers." He frowned. "I'm a rookie." He glanced warily at Sonia. "We're not really supposed to be letting anyone into the café right now. I can let Gina go in because she needs to change her clothes, but I'm not supposed to let anyone else go in."

"Right, Officer Parkers." Nikki smiled and kept a polite tone. "My friend here has been through a very traumatic experience. I don't think she wants to have a police officer hanging over her shoulder as she changes her clothes. So, I will stay with her, and we will hand the clothes right over to you, okay?"

"Alright, I guess." Officer Parkers sighed as he shuffled his feet. "It's just not what I was instructed to do."

"A little flexibility goes a long way, Officer." Nikki gave his arm a light pat. "Especially at a time like this. You wouldn't want to cause an innocent witness any more stress, would you?"

"No." The officer looked down at his feet.

"Nikki, I'm going to take Princess home. I think she's had a little too much excitement." Sonia leaned close to Nikki and hugged her. As she did, she whispered in her ear, "Come to my house as soon as you can."

"I will." Nikki gave Princess a light pet, then steered Gina into the café. "Let's get this taken care of, then you can get some rest."

"Thanks, Nikki," Gina mumbled her words as she stepped into her office. "I just can't think straight." She grabbed a black bag from the closet and unzipped it on the desk in front of her. "I keep repeating things in my mind, but not the things that I need to remember."

Nikki turned away from her as she began to unbutton her blouse.

"Try not to pressure yourself."

"How can I not?" Gina groaned. "I feel like I should be able to figure out who did this, right away. I was right here, right outside most likely, when it happened."

"Don't forget, so was I." Nikki nodded. "We would have noticed something wrong, if there was something to notice."

"What are you saying?" Gina placed her blouse and pants in the plastic bag the officer had given her.

"I'm saying, it's not your fault." Nikki took the bag carefully and handed it out through the door of the office to Officer Parkers. "There you go. Now, can she head home for some rest?"

"I'm not sure, I'll ask someone." Officer Parkers grabbed the plastic bag and hurried off down the hall.

"Let's go, Gina." Nikki glanced around the desk. "Where are your car keys?"

"They should be there." Gina pointed to a key holder mounted on the wall beside the door.

"It's empty." Nikki stared at the empty pegs, then looked back at Gina. "Are you sure you didn't put them somewhere else?"

"That's where they should be." Gina's eyes widened. "That's where I put them, I know it is."

"It's okay, we'll find them." Nikki grabbed her hand.

"Uh, excuse me?" Officer Parkers cleared his throat as he stuck his head back into the hallway. "The detective would like to speak to you both."

"I don't know if I can face him again." Gina held Nikki's hand as they walked down the hallway.

"Just talk to him for a few minutes, then I'm sure that he'll let you go home." Nikki continued to search for the keys on every surface that they passed. It made her feel uneasy to think that they were missing. "Alex wouldn't have taken your keys, would he?"

"No. He had no reason to take them. It's just my car key, my house key, the key to the café and the key to the storage shed in the back. I have another one in the kitchen for him to use to access the shed." Gina squinted as they stepped out into the afternoon sun.

"What about the café?" Nikki raised an eyebrow. "How did you get in this morning?"

"Tyler came in really early this morning because he was cleaning the floors, giving them a good scrub. I gave him the spare key yesterday, so he could get in." Gina gestured toward the door. "If I had to open I would have known mine were missing first thing." She sank down into the same chair again. She picked up the cold cup of tea in front of her and took a sip.

"Thanks for your cooperation, Gina." Quinn walked up beside her. "We're working as quickly as we can. As of now, you can go home, but I'd really appreciate it if you could be available for any further questions I may have." He crouched down so that he could look straight into her eyes. "Can I count on you for that?"

"Yes, I guess." Gina set down her mug. "It's just, I know that you had a problem with Alex."

"Whatever my personal feelings were, that doesn't matter now. It's my job to find out exactly what happened to him, and make sure that his killer is put behind bars. I'm going to do just that." Quinn stood back up. "If you think of anything at all, please call me immediately." He held out a business card to her. "I don't care what time it is, day or night, I will answer."

"Okay." Gina took the card and slipped it into her pocket.

"Your purse." Nikki suddenly snapped her fingers. "I bet that's where your keys are. Where's your purse?"

"It's in my car." Gina looked over at her car. "I never keep it in the café, too many people around to walk off with it. I just take what I need inside with me and lock my purse in the car." She groaned. "I must have left my keys in it this time. Great, so now I've locked myself out of my car. I'm usually so careful, because my car is so old, you can still lock the keys inside. I can't believe how stupid I can be."

"It's not a big deal." Nikki squeezed her hand. "I often misplace my keys."

"I can see if we can open your car." Quinn offered.

"That's okay." Gina shook her head. "I probably have a spare key at home. I'll have to get the spare key to my house from my neighbor."

"I'll get Officer Parkers to give you a ride home." Quinn waved to Officer Parkers. "You can see if you can find your spare car key."

"Thank you." Gina nodded.

"I'll come with you." Nikki helped Gina to her feet.

"No, please." Gina looked at Nikki. "I know that you're trying to be helpful, but honestly I just want to be alone. I just want to go home and try and find my keys, then get into some pajamas and go to sleep. I'll be fine, I promise."

"Okay, I understand." Nikki hugged her again. "But if you need me, just call. I'll come over right away. Are you sure you don't want me to get someone to unlock the car for you, that way you don't have to worry about it?"

"No, it's okay, if I can't find my spare, I have a service that will come out to take care of it." Gina waved her hand, then sighed. "Wow, I really need to get some rest."

"All set?" Officer Parkers gestured to his car. "I can take you right home, ma'am."

"Thanks." Gina followed after the officer.

As Nikki stared after them, she felt Quinn's attention still on her. When she turned to face him, she confirmed that his eyes remained on her.

"Are you okay, Quinn?"

"Yes, I'm fine." Quinn pulled his shoulders back. "I need to interview the people from the nearby shops and houses." He pointed to a group that had gathered near the end of the alley. Nikki recognized Josh and Adam from the bakery and Jayden from the antique store. There were a few other people that Nikki didn't recognize. "I better get to work. I need to get this case solved."

"If there's anything I can do to help, just let me know." Nikki's heartbeat quickened as she recalled the way that Gina spoke to him. "Gina didn't mean anything she said you know, she's just upset."

"No, she was right." Quinn frowned. "I did judge him, likely too quickly. I just wanted to make sure she knew about his past. Can you come by tonight? All of this will be crazy, but I'll text you when I get a few minutes free."

"Sure, I can." Nikki leaned up and was about to kiss him, but then she remembered that he needed to act professional with so many officers around them. "I'll check on Spots."

"Thank you." Quinn gazed at her a moment longer, then turned back to the other officers.

Nikki walked off in the direction of Sonia's house. As she tried to sort through everything on her mind, she hoped that she would be able to figure out something, anything, that might give Quinn a clue. The thought of being so close to the murder and yet having no idea what happened, frustrated her. But made her even more determined to help find out the truth.

CHAPTER 5

Nikki reached Sonia's door and knocked on it.

"Who is it?" Sonia called out.

"Nikki."

"Get in here!" Sonia swung the door open. "I've been waiting. Is Gina okay?"

"I think so. Officer Parkers drove her home." Nikki stepped inside and reached down to pet Princess who jumped up on her legs to greet her. She immediately felt more relaxed just by seeing the small dog.

"I've been trying to work things out." Sonia pointed to a piece of paper on the coffee table in the living room. "I noticed some things that seemed off."

"Like what?" Nikki followed her into the living

room and looked down at the paper. "What is this?" She frowned as she looked over the list.

"It's a list of my possible suspects." Sonia raised her eyebrows.

"You have suspects?" Nikki glanced up at her with a faint smile. "You've been watching those detective shows again, haven't you?"

"Maybe." Sonia laughed. "The murderer needs to be caught. What if he's still in town? What if he decides to kill again?"

"You're right, the murderer does need to be caught. We should do whatever we can to help." Nikki perched on the edge of the couch. "But I don't think it's likely he will hurt anyone else. The killer is probably someone from Alex's past. He did time in prison. I'm sure he has some enemies from that."

"Yes, that's on my list." Sonia nodded as she took the paper back. "But there's also people in this town that might have been involved. I just think that we should look at all of the possibilities. It's at least a place to start. And then there's this." She pulled out her phone and showed her the picture she'd taken of the long, pole-like object in the corner of the kitchen. "Does that look like it belongs in a kitchen to you?"

Nikki studied the image. "I can't think of what it might be used for."

"Because there's no reason for it to be there." Sonia set her phone down. "Unless someone suspected they might need it for self-defense. My guess is that Alex had it there to protect himself for some reason. Maybe he had been threatened."

"Or maybe it was just because of leftover paranoia from being in prison?" Nikki stood up and began to walk back and forth. Princess paced by her side. "Although, I think it's possible that he was aware of a threat against his life. When I met him this morning, he seemed so calm, but he backed away from Quinn very quickly. To be fair, Quinn was quite rude to him."

"Quinn?" Sonia narrowed her eyes. "That doesn't sound like our Quinn."

"No, it doesn't." Nikki smiled at her use of the word 'our'. "Did you notice anything else while you were in there?"

"This." Sonia picked up her phone and scrolled to the picture of the piece of paper that had a number on it, then held it up for Nikki to see.

"What's that?" Nikki looked at it.

"It was written on a pad of paper by the phone

in the kitchen at the café." Sonia nodded. "I was waiting for you before I called the number."

"Wait a minute, you photographed this at the crime scene?" Nikki's eyes widened as she looked up at Sonia.

"I did. I left the paper there, but I snapped a picture of the number." Sonia shrugged as she stood up from the couch. "Are you going to call it?" She held out her phone.

"I guess we should. It might have been the last thing that Alex wrote down, or the last person that he spoke to." Nikki took out her phone and made sure that her number wouldn't show, then she dialed the number from the picture. She put the phone on speaker, so that they could both hear.

"Licensing and zoning, this is Garrett."

Nikki's heart skipped a beat. She tried to think of something to say, but no words came to mind.

"Wrong number!" Sonia blurted out, then ended the call. "Are you okay, Nikki?"

"I'm sorry, I blanked. I overheard a man arguing on the phone this morning about something to do with the licensing department, I just didn't expect that to be who answered the phone." Nikki put down her phone. "So, obviously Gina has been having some trouble with them, too. I doubt it could have anything to do with Alex's death."

"Yes, it does seem like a dead end. But it was worth a try I guess." Sonia shook her head. "What we really need is to know more about Alex. Without some idea of his past, we're not going to be able to figure out who he might have been afraid of, and since he was fairly new in town, I doubt there's anyone we can find out much from."

"There's one person." Nikki bit into her bottom lip. "But I'm not sure he's going to be willing to help."

"Quinn?" Sonia met her eyes.

"Yes. I got the feeling that he could tell a lot about Alex's past just from looking at him, and I'm sure he's done some deeper research since then." Nikki crossed her arms. "But how am I going to explain to him that we're snooping around the murder."

"It's not like it's the first time. He might not like it, but he'll be expecting it." Sonia smiled at her. "I have confidence in you."

"Let's hope you're right." Nikki gave her a warm hug, then bent down to give Princess a kiss and a cuddle goodbye.

Instead of heading in the direction of her

apartment, she walked into the center of town to the police station. If Quinn was going to have a few minutes, she knew that she had to go to him. When he worked a case, he didn't have time for extra trips and seeing him face to face was the best option.

Nikki smiled and nodded to a few of the officers she passed as she headed straight to his office in the back. She'd become a familiar enough face that no one questioned her presence at the police station anymore. She spotted Quinn through the window of his office, hunched over his desk. In his late twenties he was one of the youngest detectives on the force, but at times he wore such a serious expression that to Nikki he looked far older.

As Nikki watched him, he glanced up and met her eyes through the window. A small smile appeared on his lips as he motioned her inside.

"I know you're busy." Nikki hesitated as she stood in the doorway of his office.

"It's alright, come in." Quinn gestured for her to sit in the chair in front of his desk. "Just give me a minute, I'm looking for a certain piece of paper." He flipped through the folder on his desk, then set it aside and picked up another.

"Thanks." Nikki sat down in the chair, then

watched as he sorted through another stack of papers.

"I've been so bogged down with this case that somehow I misplaced the paperwork I needed to search Alex's apartment."

"You haven't searched it, yet?" Nikki sat back in the chair.

"We searched it already, but I really need to find the paperwork." Quinn snapped his fingers and smiled as he picked up a piece of paper. "Here it is." He set the paper down on top of the first folder, then looked across the desk at her. "How are you?"

"I'm okay. Just a little confused." Nikki frowned as she met his eyes. "I know that Alex was shot, but I don't understand how he could have been killed so quietly. I mean there's quite a bit of traffic noise in the area, but still."

"The lack of sound struck me as odd, too. I think that a silencer must have been used. That would have muffled the sound. I really can't talk about this too much." Quinn met her eyes. "Aren't there other things that you could be concentrating on?"

"Yes, there are. But I just really want to know what happened to Alex, especially since I was there and I'm friends with Gina." Nikki sat forward slightly. "You told me that he was in prison. But I don't know what he was in prison for, or how long he was there."

"Most of this information is available to anyone that knows where to look, but please don't go spreading it around." Quinn flipped open a file on his desk.

"Of course, I won't."

"Let's see what I can tell you." Quinn looked over the file. "He was in prison for armed robbery, in which the victim was injured. He was in prison for ten years and was released just over a month ago." He read through the file. "According to the notes in his file, he had a few fights while on the inside, and a history of violent acts that predated his arrest."

"A few fights? Maybe he created some enemies inside?" Nikki frowned. "You don't think it was a random act, do you?"

"Not at all. I know that there are people in the community that might be afraid, but this was a targeted murder." Quinn winced as his phone started to ring. "I have to get this, Nikki. Thanks for stopping by."

Nikki started to stand up and turn toward the door.

"We'll try catch up tonight, alright?" Quinn

called out before he answered the call.

"Sure." Nikki glanced over her shoulder and smiled.

Quinn pressed the phone against his ear, then turned away as she stepped out through the door.

CHAPTER 6

*L*ater that evening, Nikki walked toward Quinn's house with Spots. He'd sent her a text in the middle of her evening walk with the dogs to let her know that he was home and he'd see her when she brought Spots back. The thought of seeing him made her quicken her step.

"Spots, Daddy's waiting for us." Nikki looked down at the dog, who seemed far more interested in the cracks in the sidewalk than getting home.

She walked up to the front door and swung it open.

"Quinn?"

Spots barked, and ran straight for Quinn, who stood not far from the door.

"Hey, buddy." Quinn smiled as he greeted the Dalmatian with a flurry of pets and kissing noises. "Did you have a good walk? Did you hunt down any innocent squirrels?"

"He got spooked by Jimmy's cat, again." Nikki laughed a little as she recalled the sheer terror in Spots' howl when the cat bolted in his direction.

"Aw, did the mean kitty scare you?" Quinn frowned as he straightened up and Spots ran over to his water bowl. "I'm going to have to have a talk with Jimmy about letting that felonious feline roam free all the time."

"Are you really?" Nikki grinned as he wrapped his arms around her waist.

"I can't have her terrorizing my pup, now can I?" Quinn gazed into Nikki's eyes. "Wow, it's so good to see you."

"It hasn't been that long." Nikki smiled as he kissed her.

"It doesn't matter how long, every time I see you, it's good to see you." Quinn brushed her hair back away from her face and stole another quick kiss. "I just got home, and I might not be here long. I'm waiting for some information to come in from the lab."

"I'll get you something to snack on, you never eat enough when you work a case." Nikki untangled from his arms and headed for the kitchen.

"You don't have to do that, you know." Quinn followed her into the kitchen as he took off his suit jacket. "I should be the one getting you a snack."

"I can do it." Nikki shrugged as she rummaged in his fridge. "It's not a big deal."

"I got you those grapes that you like." Quinn smiled.

"Great." Nikki looked for the grapes. "They are so delicious."

"Yes, thanks to you I'm addicted now." Quinn leaned back against the counter beside the fridge as she pulled out the grapes and a jug of lemonade.

"So?" Nikki rinsed the grapes off and piled them into a bowl.

"So?" Quinn watched her as he loosened his tie.

"What did you find out?" Nikki poured him a glass of lemonade, then set it down on the kitchen table. "Do you have any leads?"

"It's a little early in the investigation to say." Quinn picked up the glass, took a sip, then met her eyes. "However, I did hear about one of the rookie cops getting pushed around by my girlfriend." He raised an eyebrow. "Would you know anything about that?"

"I didn't push him around." Nikki took a quick breath. "I just made sure that Gina could have some privacy while she changed. Is that so bad?" She poured herself a glass of lemonade, too. She set the pitcher down, then looked up at him again. "I didn't get him into any trouble, did I?"

"Just the usual teasing. Now, Sonia on the other hand, she managed to invade a crime scene." Quinn walked around the side of the table and softened his voice. "I know today was rough. Gina lost a friend, but you were there, too. I know it has to be bothering you."

"It is." Nikki nodded. "I just can't believe I didn't hear anything, didn't see anything. How is that possible?"

"My guess is, he was taken by surprise. He didn't have a chance to cry out. There weren't any signs of a struggle." Quinn took a sip of his lemonade. "I think the murderer took him by surprise and shot him straight away. There must have been a silencer. And the traffic noise would have drowned it out even more. None of the people that work or live near the alley heard or saw anything, either."

"I'm sorry for the way Gina spoke to you today. She didn't mean what she said."

"Maybe she did." Quinn sighed. "Maybe she wasn't wrong, either."

"What?" Nikki met his eyes as Spots ran over to his water bowl. "What do you mean? You're a great detective."

"Maybe. Sometimes." Quinn frowned, then pursed his lips. "What she said about me not liking Alex, about me judging him because of the tattoo on his arm. She wasn't wrong. Maybe if I had paid closer attention to who he was, instead of making assumptions, I would have noticed that something was off. Maybe he needed help, and my attitude toward him prevented him from asking for it."

"Quinn." Nikki met his eyes. "You couldn't have known what was about to happen. Maybe you made an assumption, but you made it based on experience. You knew the kinds of crimes he'd committed, and you didn't want Gina, or anyone else in our town to be at risk."

"But he did his time." Quinn pulled his tie free of his collar and tossed it aside. "And now, he's paid the ultimate price. For what? For cooking at a little café?" He shook his head, then sat down in one of the chairs at the kitchen table. "The list of potential suspects is honestly endless. Ex-cons, so many of them have so many skeletons in their past, it's almost impossible to narrow it down. People he hurt when he committed his crimes, people he crossed while he was in prison, family members on the outside that he disappointed." He looked up at her, his brow furrowed. "It may only be the first day of the investigation but I really have very little to go on. I didn't even recover the murder weapon."

"It's just the beginning." Nikki bit into her bottom lip as she sat down beside him. She scooted her chair closer to him, then placed one hand on his knee as she leaned close. "There might be someone who saw something. I saw a couple when I was walking back to the café after picking up Princess. They were in this car driving really slow. It was strange, like they were looking for something."

"That's something." Quinn nodded and pulled out his phone. As he recorded her description of the couple and their car, his eyes narrowed. "I'm not sure if it will lead to anything, but it gives me something to chase down. Why didn't you tell me about this earlier?"

"I guess I just assumed they had nothing to do with it. I mean, they were nearby, but Alex was probably still alive at that point. I got caught up talking with Gina, and then I guess when the murder happened, it just went out of my mind." Nikki sighed. "My mind has been spinning all day."

"What about your talk with Gina? Did she say anything I should know about?" Quinn met her eyes.

"Not really. But she did mention to me that Walter had a serious problem with her hiring Alex at the café. I certainly don't think he would do anything to hurt Alex, but he may know more about him than we do." Nikki offered a faint shrug. "Other than that, I can't think of anything else."

"That's quite a bit more than I had." Quinn smiled and Spots ran over and lay down at his feet. Water dripping from his mouth.

"You couldn't dig up anything else on Alex's background?" Nikki bent down and patted Spots' head.

"Some. But not enough. A lot of the information in his file was blacked out. I've got a few requests in to get more information but that may take some time. As of now, we're done with the crime scene, which means Gina can open for business if she feels comfortable with that. The crime scene didn't give us much, and I doubt it will." Quinn rubbed behind the Dalmatian's ears. "About the only thing that I can pinpoint in this investigation so far, is the time of death. With only a small window of ten to fifteen minutes, that will help me to narrow down the suspects once I'm able to track some down." He glanced at his watch. "Speaking of which, I'd better move. I want to find out who that couple is, and what Walter has to say about Alex." He snatched his tie from the chair he'd tossed it on and wrapped it around his neck again. "Sorry, I have to go, but you can stay as long as you want."

"I'll make sure that Spots has his dinner." Nikki straightened his collar.

"I'll catch up with you later." Quinn kissed her cheek, then stepped out the door and closed it behind him. Nikki turned around to see Spots walking toward her with his bowl clamped between his teeth.

"Okay, okay." Nikki laughed as she followed him back into the kitchen.

Once Spots ate his food, she played with his rope with him for a bit. Then threw a ball outside for him to chase after. He seemed to have boundless energy. When he finally ran straight past her into the house with the ball in his mouth, she knew she had worn him out.

Spots ran over and plopped down in his bed with a sigh. Nikki double checked he had enough water, then gave him a kiss goodbye and locked up the house.

CHAPTER 7

Nikki stepped into her apartment and sank down on her couch. She glanced around the small apartment she'd lived in since she graduated from high school and tried to picture living somewhere else. Sure, the lack of space could be annoying sometimes, but she'd also painted every wall, selected every piece of furniture, and artwork. It had been her place of solace for a very long time. She was eager to get her own property with an animal rescue shelter, but until then she was comfortable in her surroundings.

The ring of her cell phone snapped her out of her thoughts. She snatched it up and answered it the moment that she saw Gina's name on the screen.

"Gina, is everything okay?"

"I'm not sure." Gina's voice trembled. "I'm at home, but I feel like someone is watching me, Nikki. I think someone is outside the house."

"What? Did you see anyone?" Nikki jumped to her feet.

"No, I keep looking out the window, but I don't see anyone." Gina gulped. "I feel like I'm losing it, Nikki."

"Did you call the police?" Nikki grabbed her keys and headed for the door.

"No, what if it's just my imagination?" Gina sighed. "I don't know what to say. I think someone is outside? They won't believe me."

"Hang up right now and call the police, Gina. I'm heading right over, but make sure you call them, okay? Lock your doors, stay inside. Stay away from the windows." Nikki's heart slammed against her chest as she hurried to her car.

"Please hurry, Nikki," Gina mumbled into the phone right before the call cut off.

Nikki could only hope that she would call the police as instructed. As she drove through town she felt as if she couldn't get to her friend's house fast enough. When she finally pulled into the driveway, a patrol car pulled in right behind her.

Nikki ran to the door as the officer stepped out

of his car. She recognized him from the crime scene that morning but didn't know his name.

"Gina?" She pounded on the front door. "Gina, it's me, and the police. Open the door!"

Gina opened the door just enough to see Nikki, then peered past her at the officer. "Are you sure it's safe?"

"I'll take a look around, ma'am." The officer nodded to her, then walked around the side of the house.

"Stay here with me." Nikki led Gina toward the patrol car. "Tell me what happened. Did you hear something? Did you see someone moving around?"

"I heard a thump." Gina looked fearfully toward the backyard. "I thought someone was right by the back door, but when I looked, no one was there. I don't know. I haven't been able to settle down."

"It's okay." Nikki hugged her. "You're safe now. No one is going to hurt you."

"Well, I found something." The officer rounded the other side of the house and walked up to them with his phone in his hand.

"Who was it?" Nikki's eyes widened. "Did they get away?"

"Not so much a who." The officer held up his phone

to reveal a picture of a raccoon digging through Gina's trash. "It looks like you have a hungry critter on your hands." He smiled as he looked up from the phone. "Nothing to worry about too much, though. I scared him off." He tucked his phone back into his pocket.

"Oh wow, I'm so embarrassed." Gina winced and covered her face. "I'm so sorry. I could have sworn someone was out there."

"It's alright." The officer shrugged. "After a murder like what happened at your café today it's very common to be frightened when you're alone. Do you have anyone who can stay with you?"

"My boyfriend, Mario, is on his way." Gina nodded, then frowned. "I'm so sorry for calling you out here."

"Don't be." The officer looked from her to Nikki, then back at Gina. "Don't hesitate to call again. Right now, we have a murderer at large. It's not likely that the killer will come back, but it's okay to be cautious just in case." He nodded to both of them, then climbed back into his car.

"Nikki, I'm so sorry." Gina shook her head. "I guess I really am losing it."

"I don't think you're losing it." Nikki hugged her. "I'll stay with you until Mario gets here, okay?

Have you two been together long?" She was surprised Gina hadn't mentioned him before.

"Thank you." Gina led her back toward the house. "No, we haven't been. We've been dating for almost a month. Come inside, I'll tell you all about him, the least I can do is offer you some tea."

"No, thanks." Nikki followed her inside. "If you don't mind, I'd like to take a look around outside."

"Sure, that's fine." Gina flashed a smile over her shoulder. "Just watch out for those scary raccoons." She rolled her eyes.

Gina's house was small, two bedrooms, one bathroom, with a small, screened-in porch on the back. Nikki had been to it a few times over the span of their friendship. A little overgrown in some places, she could easily see how someone might be able to sneak around in the yard. Straggly bushes along the property line served as the only barrier between her yard and the one behind it.

Nikki eyed the back door, where Gina had claimed to hear a thump. Sure, it could have been the sound of the raccoon knocking off the trash can lid, but it could also have been something else. She swept her gaze along the two stone steps that led up to the back door beside the porch. With the beam of the flashlight on her phone, she did her best to reveal every inch of the door and the area that surrounded it. As she noticed some dirt in a scattered pile near the back door, she heard a scuffling sound behind her.

Nikki spun around and pointed the flashlight in the direction of the sound. As she did, she revealed a face between two of the scraggly bushes.

"You stop right there!" Nikki shouted as the man started to back up.

He bumped into a woman who stood a few inches away from him. Nikki squinted at them both as she approached them. She wanted to remember every detail of their faces.

"What are you doing here?"

"Nothing, honest." The man held up his hands. His lean frame was softer than muscular, while his face had a doughy roundness to it. The woman beside him was as angular as he was round, and about a couple of inches shorter than him. They looked to be in their fifties.

"We just came to see what was happening." The woman took a step forward. "We saw the lights, heard the sirens." She frowned as she looked down at her feet. "We were just curious."

"We live next door." The man draped his arm

around the woman's shoulders. "We're sorry, we didn't mean to cause any trouble for anyone."

"You startled me." Nikki lowered her phone. "Did you happen to notice anyone in the yard earlier?"

"No one." The woman shook her head. "It's been quiet. That's why we were so surprised when we saw the police lights. We just wanted to make sure that everyone was okay."

"Well, if you could let me know if you notice anything out of the ordinary, I would really appreciate it. Gina has been through a lot." Nikki pulled a card from her pocket and handed it to the man.

"You're a dog walker?" He looked up from the card.

"Yes, but you can reach me any time on that number." Nikki glanced back toward the front of the house as she noticed a flash of lights in the driveway. When she turned back to the couple, she found that they had already disappeared.

Surprised, she looked past the bushes for any sign of them. She guessed they were embarrassed that they'd been caught being nosy.

Nikki couldn't blame them, she was just as nosy.

But something told her that the pair weren't being completely honest with her.

She walked back to the front of the house and spotted a man as he walked toward the front door. He had a large dog on a leash beside him.

"Mario?"

He turned to look at her and offered a light smile and nod. "That's me. And you are?"

"Nikki." She offered her hand to him as she joined him on the walkway.

"The dog walker, right?" Mario shook her hand. "Gina has told me a lot about you."

"Oh?" Nikki quirked an eyebrow as the front door swung open. "Aren't you a beauty." She bent down to pat the black Labrador's head. He wagged his tail with excitement.

"This is Bentley." Mario smiled at the dog.

"Oh, he's a beauty." Nikki continued to pat him.

"Mario, thanks so much for coming over." Gina waved her hand. "It's just me being ridiculous. The police have already searched the yard." She winced. "You must think I'm such a wuss to be afraid to be alone."

"Not at all." Mario hugged her. "As long as you need me, I'm happy to be at your side."

Nikki's heart warmed at the sight of the two locked in an embrace.

"Come inside." Gina held the door open for both of them. She patted Bentley's head on the way inside. "Did you find anything, Nikki?"

"No, nothing. I'm sorry, Gina." Nikki considered mentioning her neighbors but guessed that their nosiness might upset her.

"I'm sorry I wasn't there when you closed the café. You know I like to be there." Mario sat down on the couch beside Gina. "Everybody knows that closing time is when robbers might attack. What if you forgot to lock the door?"

"I didn't." Gina sighed. "The front door was locked. Maybe that's why Alex was attacked in the alley."

"No, it wasn't locked." Nikki settled in a chair across from the couch. Bentley ran over to her and sat down in front of her. She leaned forward and patted his head.

"Of course, it was locked. I'd already closed up for the day." Gina frowned as she looked at Nikki. "Why would you say it wasn't?"

"Because I found you in Woof Way. But when Sonia arrived, she went inside to make us tea, and she just walked through the door. It wasn't locked.

At least not then." Nikki rubbed her hand along Bentley's back as he lay down at her feet.

"That seems impossible." Gina narrowed her eyes. "Maybe the police left it unlocked after they conducted their initial search."

"Maybe." Nikki nodded. "Speaking of locks, did you get your car unlocked okay?"

"Luckily, I found my spare key that I had tucked away and I unlocked it." Gina rubbed her forehead. "But unfortunately my keys weren't in it. Honestly, I haven't looked too hard for them, I've been so preoccupied with everything."

"I'm sorry, Gina. Now that Mario's here, I hope that you'll feel a little more secure." Nikki shifted her gaze to Mario. She recalled asking Gina if she and Alex were in a relationship. No wonder her friend had been a little offended. "I'm sorry we had to meet this way, Mario, but I'm glad you're here. And Bentley, too, of course."

"Me too. Bentley likes you." Mario smiled at the dog as he continued to lie down at Nikki's feet. "Don't worry, I'll keep a close eye on her. Until all of this is over, I'm not letting her out of my sight."

"Oh, please don't say that." Gina shook her head. "You know that I like my alone time."

"Sorry." Mario looked into her eyes. "I'm not

going to let anything happen to you. You have no idea how scared I was when I found out what happened today. That could have been you dead in that alley."

"But it wasn't me." Gina leaned her head against his shoulder. "It was Alex."

Mario flexed one hand, then curved it into a fist that rested against his thigh.

Nikki noticed some bruising on the back of his hand.

"Did you hurt yourself?" She pointed to the marks.

"Oh, no." Mario frowned. "Just lost my temper."

"You had your reasons." Gina kissed his cheek. "Let's not dwell on it now, alright?"

"You're right." Mario nodded, then sprawled his hand out again.

Nikki studied the bruises. What could have caused Mario to lose his temper, and why was Gina so forgiving of it? She knew that Gina hated violence. Would she really be interested in someone who lost his temper and apparently punched things? Or people? Her heart skipped a beat at the thought.

"Where were you today, Mario?" Nikki asked as

Bentley looked up at her, then rolled over onto his back. She rubbed his belly.

"Huh?" Mario glanced over at her.

"I mean, when all of this happened. You said that you liked to be there when Gina closes up, but you weren't there today, were you working?" Nikki tried to sound casual. She noticed Gina sit up and straighten her shoulders.

"I'm a consultant for a security firm." Mario cleared his throat. "My hours are always changing based on what a particular client needs."

"Besides, as I've told him, I don't need someone there to protect me. I'm rarely ever there alone. My cook, or my busboy, or one of the waitstaff are usually always there to close up with me. Besides, I don't need someone to take care of me." Gina frowned as she looked at Nikki. "It's not his fault that he wasn't there."

"Of course, it wasn't. I'm sorry, I didn't mean to imply that it was." Nikki's tone softened as she heard the frustration in her friend's voice. "This day has me pretty frazzled."

"You should go home and get some rest, Nikki. Now that Mario is here, I know that I'll be able to sleep." Gina stood up and walked over to Nikki as she stood up. She gave Nikki a hug. "Thanks so much for being here and looking out for me. I really appreciate it."

"Anytime, Gina." Nikki bent down to say goodbye to Bentley. "Hopefully, I'll see you again soon." She patted his head. Bentley barked once as if he was agreeing with her.

On her drive home Nikki decided that Gina had the right idea, a good night's rest was what she needed as well.

When Nikki got inside her small apartment, she turned her phone volume to low and sprawled out in her bed. The familiar surroundings of her apartment gave her some comfort. From her bed she could see just about every area of her home. There weren't many places that a person could sneak in. She drifted off to sleep with the events of the day running through her mind.

CHAPTER 8

When Nikki woke the next morning, she found several texts from Quinn asking if she was awake, if she could talk, if he could come over. She sighed as she sent him an apology for missing them. Before she could put her phone down, it rang. Instead of Quinn, Sonia's name bounced across the screen.

"Good morning, Sonia." Nikki put her on speakerphone and pulled on some fresh clothes as they exchanged greetings. She filled her in on what had happened at Gina's.

"Poor girl. She must be on edge." Sonia sighed. "I'm sure she was scared."

"She was, but she felt better once Mario

arrived." Nikki pulled her hair back into a ponytail. "Have you met him?"

"Yes, twice. When I stopped in for a coffee to go. His dog is so cute, a bit nervous of Princess, though." Sonia laughed. "Mario seems like a nice, young man. A bit jealous, though."

"Jealous?" Nikki picked up the phone and carried it into the kitchen with her. "What do you mean?"

"He didn't seem to like Alex much. If Alex came out to ask Gina a question, Mario would clam right up, but as soon as Alex was gone, he would be friendly again."

"Interesting." Nikki grabbed a bottle of juice from the fridge and a blueberry muffin from the bread box. "I'm on my way to pick up Princess."

"While you two take your walk, I'm going into town to meet with a friend of mine. She must have heard something about Alex's past because she's been posting about knowing about his past on the community page, and I want to know more. She hasn't posted anything specific, but I want to speak to her about it."

"Okay, I'm heading out now. You can go ahead if you want, I'll only be a few minutes." Nikki ended the call, then tucked her phone into her pocket.

As Nikki walked toward Sonia's house, she ate her muffin, and tried to evaluate what she'd learned about Alex the day before. She wanted to see if she could find out anything else about Alex's connections and his murder. She decided to start by trying to find out more about Walter.

Nikki arrived at Sonia's house and noticed that her car wasn't in the driveway. Assuming she already went into town, she let herself into the house with her key.

Princess greeted her with her usual excitement. Nikki bent down so that Princess could lick her cheeks. There was nothing like the love and affection of a dog to start the day off right. It immediately helped Nikki relax.

"Hi sweetie. We're going to walk a different way today." Nikki snapped on Princess' leash, then led her down the driveway.

Instead of their usual path, Nikki walked toward an address she'd looked up the night before. It didn't take long to get onto the street she needed, and after that it was a matter of counting down house numbers. When she paused in front of the house she sought, she spotted a man on his front porch.

"Walter?" Nikki smiled as she waved to him. "Is that you?"

Walter stared at her as she walked up his driveway.

"What are you doing here?" He glared. Nikki was surprised at his reaction. He was usually a relaxed and welcoming man.

"Just passing by." Nikki shrugged. "Is everything okay?"

"I want to know what you're doing here." Walter crossed his arms as he continued to glare at her.

"I was just taking Princess for a walk." Nikki pasted a warm smile across her lips. "This little girl has such a mind of her own, she tugs me everywhere."

"I don't buy it." Walter stomped one foot against the faded wood of the porch. "Princess just happens to be interested in my property?"

"Oh, I think she just misses seeing your pup. Is he inside?" Nikki picked up Princess and climbed the first step that led up to the porch. Walter had an energetic Boxer, Duke, that Princess got along with, even though he was much larger than her. They often saw each other at Gina's café.

"I said go." Walter snarled his words.

"Alright, alright." Nikki stepped back down,

then frowned. "I'm sorry, I didn't mean to cause you any trouble. I just thought we'd say hello." She set Princess back down on the ground. "We've missed seeing you at the café."

"Yes, well after what happened there, yesterday, I'm quite glad that I wasn't there. Gina made her choice when she told me I wasn't welcome." Walter frowned as his arms dropped down to his sides. "All I tried to do was give her some friendly advice, and she turned on me."

"I'm sorry to hear that. I know she's been under some stress lately." Nikki looked into his eyes. "Do you think maybe she was just having a bad morning when you spoke to her?"

"No, I don't think so. I think she wanted me off of her property, out of her café, which is what she told me. I warned her that Alex was no good, but she didn't want to hear it. I've been going to her café for years, and she kicked me out because I told her the truth about the criminal she hired." Walter rolled his eyes. "Then she must have told the police about that, too, because next thing I knew that detective boyfriend of yours was here knocking on the door."

"Yes, he's investigating the murder." Nikki

nodded. "I'm sure you'd like to see that crime solved, too."

"Of course, I would. No one wants to have a murder happen in their neighborhood. But the truth is, this is Gina's fault. She brought this element into her café, into our neighborhood, and she knew that something like this was going to happen." Walter pursed his lips.

"She couldn't have known." Nikki frowned. "How could she have possibly known that something like this would happen? Alex didn't hurt anyone, he's the one who was murdered."

"She knew, because I warned her. People with a past, it always comes back to haunt them. Usually it haunts the people around them, too. That's why it's better to stay away from them." Walter sighed as he held out his hand to Princess.

Princess made her way up the steps to sniff his hand.

As Nikki watched Walter pet Princess, she wondered if that was why he stayed to himself so much. Did he think it was safer that way? She had a hunch and she wanted to see how it played out.

"I've heard some rumors about your history." Nikki watched as he stood up and narrowed his eyes. "You don't have to worry about it, though, that's in the past, it makes no difference to me. I would never hold that against you. I know that things happen in life. I know that you can't judge someone by their past. You've always been kind to me. That's all I need to know."

"Is that what you think?" Walter straightened up and continued to look into her eyes. "Forgive and forget? You know what I call that?"

"What?" Nikki braced herself as his tone grew more tense. She'd taken a chance by guessing that he might have a criminal past of his own, and so far it seemed that she was right.

"Ignorance." Walter pointed his finger at her. "A tiger doesn't change its spots. That's what people don't understand."

"Stripes," Nikki mumbled, then took a breath. "But you have, haven't you, Walter?"

"There are some exceptions but that doesn't change the fact that most people aren't going to change. If Alex had lived long enough, he would have eventually gotten caught up in something illegal again. It was only a matter of time." Walter leaned against the porch railing and stared down at her. "You're so young, aren't you? What are you? Nineteen? Twenty?"

"Older than that." Nikki frowned. "I'm almost twenty-five."

"So young." Walter ran his hand back through his hair. "I can't explain things like this to you, because you can't possibly understand. But heed my advice, stay away from people with a past. Even if they have good intentions, things always end up getting messed up."

"Is that what happened to you, Walter?" Nikki raised an eyebrow. "Did things get messed up for you when Alex showed up?"

"I don't know what you mean." Walter crossed his arms again. "Like I said, you should go."

"It wasn't about Gina's safety, or the safety of our town, was it?" Nikki locked her eyes to his. "Alex knew something about you. Or he reminded you of something. I think that you couldn't stand him being here, because it meant that you could no longer ignore your past. So, what was it? What happened between the two of you in the past?"

"I'm not saying anything else to you." Walter's eyes narrowed as his voice grew rough. "You need to leave me alone."

Nikki's heart skipped a beat as she saw an expression cross his features that she didn't recognize. The coldness in his eyes made her shiver.

She picked Princess up in her arms and backed away from the porch.

"Hiding from it won't change anything, Walter. If you need my help with anything, you know where you can find me." She smiled. "Maybe Princess and Duke can play together sometime."

"Stay out of all of this, Nikki, if you know what's best for you, you'll listen to me." Walter called out.

"I'm going to do what I can to try and help figure out who the murderer is, Walter." Nikki did her best to sound casual. "Like I said, contact me if you need anything." She quickened her pace. "Let's go, Princess."

CHAPTER 9

Nikki's heart still raced as she arrived back at Sonia's house. Just as Nikki unlocked the front door, Sonia's car pulled up in the driveway.

"Nikki." Sonia stepped out of the car. "I have something to tell you!"

"Me too." Nikki held the door open for her. "I think Walter is definitely hiding something."

"Walter?" Sonia raised her eyebrows. "I agree. In fact, my friend told me that she overheard Walter and Alex arguing. Walter accused him of being a snitch and warned him not to tell anyone about things they did in the past."

"I knew it!" Nikki snapped her fingers, then she let Princess off her leash. "He and Alex must have committed some crime together. And Walter doesn't want it brought up again. Did she say what?"

"She claims she doesn't know. But I'm not sure she was telling me everything." Sonia frowned.

"Maybe we can see if she'll tell us more if we talk to her again." Nikki pulled out her phone. "I'm not sure if Quinn found out anything from Walter. So, if Walter and Alex have a past connection, maybe Alex threatened to out him to the town. Maybe he was blackmailing Walter."

"Maybe." Sonia pursed her lips. "It just doesn't seem like Walter, does it?"

"I also didn't think he was a criminal." Nikki shook her head. "Sometimes people can portray one image and be completely different. Unfortunately, until we can find out more about Walter or Alex, this information kind of leads us right back to a dead end." She looked over at Sonia. "I'm going to take Princess for another walk, not a long one. I cut her walk a little short and she's still full of energy."

"I'll join you." Sonia nodded. "Why don't we go near the café. Maybe, being in the area will help us piece some of these ideas together."

"Good idea." Nikki smiled.

As they walked toward the café, Nikki

mentioned the information that Quinn shared with her.

"Why do you think so much of Alex's file is blacked out?" Nikki pulled back on Princess' leash as she sniffed a bush.

"If Walter accused Alex of being a snitch, maybe he also gave information to the police about other criminals?" Sonia lowered her voice as they neared the café. "I'm sure the police would try to keep that information from being made public, or it would make Alex a target."

"If he did turn in other criminals, then there might be quite a few with an ax to grind." Nikki paused on the sidewalk. "Let's look around the area."

"That's a good idea, maybe something will jog your memory." Sonia quickened her pace to keep up with her.

"Gina and I were in front of the café, which means the murderer had to run out through the back, so let's start there. Maybe they left something behind. Although, I doubt it, I'm sure the police would have got all of the evidence by now. But it's still worth having a look." Nikki pointed to an assortment of gardens that backed up to a narrow, overgrown path that ran behind the line of shops that faced the main street. "As soon as the killer stepped out of the alley, he or she would have faced this. So, where would they have gone?" She narrowed her eyes as she looked over the options.

Sonia rubbed her forearms, then frowned as she studied the backs of the houses.

"It's hard for me to believe that no one saw anything. Someone must have been home."

"It's possible that someone did see something but they didn't realize it was important. It probably didn't seem unusual to anyone to see someone stroll by. But I'm surprised Gina and I didn't see anyone." Nikki sighed as she surveyed the options. "Which way would the murderer use to escape. If it was me, I think I would want to avoid the streets in the immediate vicinity. I think I would also want to avoid a house that looked occupied. Too much chance of someone spotting me. So, if that was the case, then I'd probably head toward this house." She traversed an overgrown path and walked past a house not far from the back of the café. The grass was overgrown, and a pile of debris near the back porch indicated it likely hadn't been occupied for some time. "And there's a path that heads straight to the front of the house and out to the street. It would mean I could run straight through." As she stopped to look more closely Princess started tugging her into the grass.

"Out of there, Princess!" Sonia demanded.

"Oh, maybe she can smell something?" Nikki watched Princess as she began to pull harder at the end of the leash and started digging in the overgrown garden. "You better take her. I don't want her to get hurt." She handed Sonia the leash.

"Come here, baby." Sonia bent down and picked Princess up. She stroked Princess' fur as she watched her friend. "Nikki, be careful." She frowned and stepped closer to the edge of the yard. "Who knows what might be hiding in there?"

Nikki crouched down where Princess had been digging in the thick, overgrown bush. She did her best to ignore the possibilities of what might crawl on her as she dug her hands into the thick branches of the bush. Her fingertips bumped into something solid, cool, and smooth. Her stomach twisted both in anticipation and fear as she discovered a handle.

"I've got something!" Nikki yanked the object out of the tangled branches of the bush and stood up. As she thrust it into the air to get a better look at it in the sunlight, she heard someone shout.

"Drop the weapon!"

Another voice chimed in. "Place the gun on the ground and put your hands up!"

Nikki swallowed hard as her first instinct was to spin around to face the people who issued the commands, however she knew that might look threatening to them. Instead, she forced herself to raise the hand without the gun and bend down and put the gun on the ground, then raised her other hand into the air as well.

"Step away from the gun." A woman's voice instructed.

Nikki took a step back from the gun and finally braved a look over her shoulder. Two people in suits, the same people that she'd seen driving slowly by the café the day before, had their guns pointed at her.

"She hasn't done anything wrong!" Sonia shouted from the sidewalk. "Put those guns away!"

"It's okay, Sonia." Nikki did her best to keep her voice calm. She didn't want anything she did to put Sonia at risk. "Just try to stay calm."

"Get down on your knees." The man commanded her.

"Not until you identify yourselves!" Nikki kept her hands in the air. "I know my rights."

"We're federal agents." The woman shouted. "Now, get down on your knees!"

Nikki's heart raced. The FBI? What business did they have with her? The thought of being in FBI custody sent her mind spinning into a panic. She eased herself down onto her knees.

"This is all a misunderstanding, please, just listen to me."

"You can tell us all about it." The man yanked her hands down behind her back and clasped handcuffs over her wrists.

"Please, I am only trying to help. I think I found the murder weapon." Nikki tipped her head toward the gun on the ground. "It's right there. I'm sure it's the gun that killed Alex."

"Are you?" The woman helped her to her feet. "Well, the only person who could be absolutely sure of that is Alex's killer."

"What?" Nikki looked at her with wide eyes. "You think I'm his killer?"

"That's ridiculous! Nikki, I'm calling Quinn right now." Sonia huffed as she pulled out her phone.

"Ma'am, keep your distance." The man warned her.

"Do you have any weapons on you right now?" The woman began to search Nikki.

"No, I don't have any weapons." Nikki could barely form the words as her mind sorted through what had happened. Would she really be arrested for Alex's murder? The woman turned her around to face both of them.

"We have some questions that you're going to need to answer. We're going to take you to the local police station to discuss this." She nodded to the man beside her. "This is Agent Daniels, and I'm Agent Perry." They held out their badges.

"Please, there's no need for this. I'll answer any questions you might have." Nikki looked between the two of them as her heart raced. The truth was, she had a lot of questions of her own that she wanted answered.

"Great, then we shouldn't have any trouble." Agent Perry hooked her hand around Nikki's arm and guided her toward the car at the end of the alley.

"You're making a huge mistake here!" Sonia followed after them with Princess clutched tightly in her arms. "You're arresting an innocent woman!"

"If that's the case, then we'll have it all straightened

out in no time." Agent Perry glanced over at her. "Just relax, we're going to get to the bottom of all of this, I can promise you that. We aren't arresting her."

"I need to get your details." Agent Daniels pulled out his notepad as he looked at Sonia.

After Sonia had reluctantly given her details, Nikki allowed Agent Perry to guide her into the back seat of the car.

Nikki's heart sank as she saw the fear in Sonia's eyes.

"It's alright, Sonia." She forced a smile to her lips. "I'm sure we'll all laugh about this later."

"Trust me, there's nothing to laugh about." Agent Daniels glanced back at her as he settled in the driver's seat. "The sooner you tell us the truth, the sooner we can get through all of this."

"I am telling you the truth." Nikki leaned forward some in the back seat. "Please, I would never do anything to hurt anyone. I certainly wouldn't hurt Alex."

"According to witness testimony, you were one of the last people to see him alive." Agent Daniels drove in the direction of the police station. "You were there when his body was found."

"That may be true, but I didn't cause him any harm." Nikki tried to ignore the tightness of the handcuffs on her wrists. How long would she be in them? Would they be replaced with bars on a jail cell?

Nikki took a deep breath and reminded herself that when she arrived at the police station Quinn would be there. Surely, he would make sure that she was okay. But what if there was nothing that he could do? Her stomach churned as the car turned into the parking lot of the police station. Sudden panic caused her heart to flutter and her chest to tighten. What if she never got to leave?

CHAPTER 10

Nikki's cheeks burned as Agent Daniels led her past a gathering of police officers. She knew that most of them would recognize her, and easily notice that she was in handcuffs. How could she ever face them again after being arrested? What would they say to Quinn about her?

"We'll need to use one of your interrogation rooms." Agent Perry flashed her badge at the officer behind the desk.

"What is this all about?" The officer narrowed his eyes. "What did she do?"

"That's not your concern, Officer." Agent Daniels squinted at the officer's shirt. "Jacobson? Is that the name I should use when I write out my complaint?"

"Yes, sure, you can use it." The officer glared at him. "Right after you tell me why you've got her in handcuffs." He looked at the other officers near the front desk. "Someone better get Quinn in here right away."

Nikki chewed on her bottom lip as she felt the tension increase between Officer Jacobson and the FBI agents. She had no idea what might happen, but she was certain that Quinn would not be pleased.

"A room, like I asked for." Agent Perry raised her voice.

"There." The officer pointed down the hall. "First door on your right." He stepped out from behind the long desk. "But I will set her up in there." He wrapped his hand around Nikki's arm.

Although she didn't know him very well, she felt intense gratitude as he escorted her toward the room. At the very least he was making an effort to protect her.

"What's happened?" The officer guided her through the door of the room, then unfastened the handcuffs, only to refasten them with her hands in front of her.

"We'll take it from here." Agent Daniels waved the officer out of the room.

"Quinn will be here soon." Officer Jacobson locked his eyes to Nikki's as he stepped out of the room. "You don't have to answer any of their questions."

"Unbelievable!" Agent Perry pushed the door shut, then turned to face Nikki. "He's right. You don't have to answer any of our questions, but it would be best if you did." She gestured to the chair behind the only table in the room. "Please, sit."

"I don't want to cause any trouble." Nikki sank down in the chair. "There's no reason to have me handcuffed."

"You'll forgive us if we can't simply trust you on that." Agent Daniels sat on the edge of the chair across from her. "Nikki, what were you doing out there today?"

"I was just having a look around. I wanted to see if anything jogged my memory. Princess, my friend's Chihuahua, started tugging and digging, so I wanted to see what she was looking for." Nikki's mouth grew dry. Was it best to tell the truth or would it only make things worse?

"I guess it was pretty easy to know where to go to look for evidence, since you're the one that hid it there." Agent Perry smiled at her as she leaned against the corner of the table beside Nikki.

"It's not like that! You have this all wrong!" Nikki raised her voice slightly as she shook her head.

"Relax." Agent Daniels commanded as he stood up. "You're not in any position to raise your voice to us!"

"I'm sorry." Nikki lowered her voice as she was reminded of the position she was in. "I don't mean any disrespect. It's just that all of this has gotten out of control. If you would let me explain, I think we could all see that this is just a mistake."

"What we see, very clearly, is that you were caught with the gun, which is most likely the murder weapon, in your hand." Agent Daniels stared straight into her eyes. "All you have to do is explain how you came to find it so easily when the police who combed the area couldn't manage to do the same."

"I just wanted to see if anything triggered my memory, so I could try and work out what had happened when Alex was murdered. We were just having a look around and Princess led me to the area where the gun was." Nikki took a slow breath.

"It sounds like you're very interested in this murder." Agent Daniels sat back down.

"I am, I was there when Gina found Alex. I want to know who did this to him." Nikki looked at Agent Daniels as he pulled out his phone.

"We're not here because of the murder, not exactly, anyway." He held up his phone to display a picture on the screen. "Recognize him?"

"That's Alex." Nikki stared at the image.

"Yes, it is." Agent Daniels flipped to another image. "How about these two, do you recognize them? They use disguises, so they might not have looked exactly the same as they do here."

Nikki squinted at the picture. She thought she had seen them before but wasn't sure.

"I think I might have seen them around, but I don't know where. I've never met them. Why? Who are they?"

"They are two people who were hunting down Alex. Maybe, one of these people came to you." Agent Daniels set his phone down and looked straight into her eyes. "Maybe he or she offered you a sizable sum of money, if you would give them a heads-up about Alex's routine. Maybe you knew where the murder weapon was, because you told them where to hide it."

"What?" Nikki's eyes widened. "You can't be serious. You think I helped them murder Alex?"

"We're not sure what to think, we're still figuring it out." Agent Perry leaned closer to her. "But in order for us to do that, you need to help us out. You claim that you had nothing to do with it, but somebody did. Probably somebody you know."

"No." Nikki stared down at the table as her eyes filled with tears. "No, I didn't have anything to do with any of it."

The door to the interrogation room opened, and Quinn stepped inside, his eyes wild as he looked around the room.

"What's going on here?"

Nikki took a sharp breath as she saw the flush in Quinn's cheeks. She could tell that he was trying to remain calm, but he was clearly upset.

"What are you doing?" Agent Daniels stood up. "You can't barge in here! We're in the middle of an interrogation!"

"I'm Detective Quinn Grant." He showed them his badge. "I need to know what is happening?" He glanced at Nikki, before turning his attention back to the FBI agents. "Neither of you is even authorized to be involved in this investigation, I haven't received any notifications about your involvement."

"Consider this your notification." Agent Perry crossed her arms as she glared at him. "And apparently it didn't come soon enough, since you seem to want to involve your personal feelings in a homicide investigation."

"You can't hold her. You have no reason to arrest her!" Quinn stared at them.

"How about the murder weapon with her fingerprints on it?" Agent Perry held up a clear, plastic bag with the gun inside. As Nikki looked at it, she realized that it had what must be a silencer attached to it. "Is that enough to arrest her?"

Quinn's flushed cheeks suddenly grew pale as he stared at the bag. He looked from it to Nikki. "Did you touch it, Nikki?"

Nikki's heart beat even faster, though she didn't think it was possible. She nodded as she stared into Quinn's eyes.

"I didn't know it was the murder weapon. Princess was digging in the bush and I felt something, and I pulled it out. I'm sorry, Quinn, I wasn't thinking." Nikki frowned as she looked down at her still handcuffed hands. Her heart sank as she realized that Quinn wasn't going to be able to set her free and might even lose his job over his desire to. "Quinn, it's okay." She looked up at him. "I don't mind answering their questions. I'll do whatever I can to help the investigation. Please, just let them do what they need to do."

"Good answer." Agent Daniels smiled as he looked from Nikki to Quinn. "Maybe take some advice from your girlfriend, I'm guessing?" He glanced between them again. "Yes, I know that look in your eyes. You're way too close to this case now, Detective Grant. Give us the room, please."

"No." Quinn pulled out one of the chairs at the table and sat down in it. "If she's going to be questioned, then I am going to be right here while you do it. Right now, this is still my investigation, and that makes her my witness, not yours. So, if you want to ask your questions, go right ahead, but I'm not leaving her alone in here with you."

Nikki closed her eyes as a wave of relief washed over her. The last thing she wanted was to be alone with two FBI agents who appeared to be convinced that she had killed Alex.

"As you may know." Agent Perry looked across the table at Quinn. "Alex had given quite a bit of information about other criminals in exchange for his early release from prison. Because of that, we knew that he could be at risk of retaliation, so we have been keeping an eye on him."

"And yet, you don't know who killed him?" Quinn looked between the two of them. "How is that possible if you were monitoring him?"

"We weren't exactly monitoring him." Agent Daniels frowned as he flipped through his phone again. "We were following two other criminals believed to have been involved in multiple jewelry robberies with Alex before he was incarcerated. We received a tip that they intended to target Alex when he was released from prison. We tracked them here." He held up his phone for Quinn to see. "Luisa and Farro Hale, a married couple, both career criminals. They are masters of disguise, so take a close look. Do you recognize them?"

"No, I don't." Quinn took the phone from the agent's hand and expanded the picture to get a closer look. "Do you think they killed him?"

"Well, we considered it." Agent Daniels took his phone back and slid it into his pocket. "However, my guess is that the Hales were after Alex to recover some stolen goods that were never recovered. The rumor is that they'd been waiting for Alex to be released from prison, so that they could get their cut."

"So, they murdered him for it?" Quinn stood up, then shrugged. "It should be a pretty open and shut case."

"Not so fast." Agent Perry glared at him. "There's no history of violence in their record. They also wouldn't kill him unless they got what they came for, and we have reason to believe that they didn't."

"What reason is that?" Quinn crossed his arms.

Nikki sank back in her chair. She did her best to memorize every word she heard exchanged between the three as it might be the most information she'd get about the case.

"Because we saw them walking toward the alley." Agent Perry cringed. "They spotted us and they managed to evade us."

"Doesn't that just prove that it could have been them?" Quinn narrowed his eyes. "Why is Nikki here if you already have two main suspects?"

"Because we saw them this morning." Agent Daniels placed his hands on the table and leaned across it to look into Nikki's eyes. "Tell me something, Nikki, why would they come back to the crime scene if they already got what they came for?"

"I don't know." Nikki shook her head.

"This isn't necessary." Quinn leaned closer to the

agents. "You don't have a reason to hold her. It's time to let her go. She obviously didn't have anything to do with this. She was with the owner of the café just before the body was discovered. She has a solid alibi for the time of death that the medical examiner has suggested. There is absolutely no way you can prove that she was involved with this crime, because she wasn't."

"Is that your unbiased opinion?" Agent Perry rolled her eyes.

"It's the truth." Nikki spoke up, her confidence bolstered by the alibi that Quinn pointed out.

"It's very simple. She's free to go. You have nothing to hold her on. We all have the same interests at heart here, don't we?" Quinn looked between the two agents. "We want to find out who killed Alex. Wasting time questioning a suspect with an alibi isn't going to get us any closer to finding that out."

"He's not wrong. We will still be investigating whether you were involved in Alex's murder." Agent Perry walked over to Nikki and unlocked the handcuffs. "But for the moment, you are free to go."

CHAPTER 11

When Agent Perry removed the handcuffs, Nikki's heart raced as she felt the freedom of her wrists.

"I'll walk you out." Quinn followed her toward the door. A burst of elation carried through her when she stepped out into the parking lot. Not long before she wondered if she would ever be able to do that. She took a breath of the fresh air.

"Nikki." Quinn looked into her eyes. "I'm sorry I didn't get here faster. I'm sorry you went through that."

"It's alright, it was no big deal." Nikki shrugged.

"Yes, it was, I know it was."

"I'm sorry, I never thought I would find the murder weapon. Princess sniffed it out." Nikki walked along the sidewalk. "I also didn't expect two FBI agents to be following me. Did you know they were here?"

"Me?" Quinn matched her pace. "I had no idea."

"Do you think the couple they are after did it?" Nikki turned to face him.

"I'm not sure. The fact that they were spotted near the crime scene this morning makes me doubt it, but I can't rule anything out." Quinn settled his hand on her shoulder. "This case is dangerous, Nikki. Alex had all kinds of enemies, the criminal type, that won't think twice about going after an innocent person who gets in their way."

"You don't have to worry about me, Quinn." Nikki smiled. "I'm fine."

"I don't?" Quinn searched her eyes. "I was more than a little worried when I saw you in handcuffs today."

"It was a misunderstanding." Nikki rubbed her hands along her wrists as she avoided his eyes.

"Quite a misunderstanding." Quinn shifted closer to her. "This is dangerous. You need to stay out of this."

"I get it, Quinn." Nikki met his eyes. "I didn't expect to find anything, especially not the murder weapon. But like I said, you don't have to worry about me."

"I hope that's true." Quinn kissed her cheek, then looked into her eyes. "I might be busy, but I'm always here for you, alright?"

"Alright." Nikki smiled. "Thanks, Quinn."

"Always." Quinn winked. "I have to go deal with these feds. I'm going to trust that you'll be safe?"

"I'll be safe." Nikki gave his hand another squeeze, then headed down the sidewalk. At the moment she wanted to get as far away from the police station as she could.

After sending a quick text to Sonia to let her know that she was okay, Nikki headed straight for the only pawn shop in town. Now that she knew that Alex had stolen jewelry in the past, maybe he tried to pawn it. Maybe he even stole more. If he needed some funds to keep him afloat, he might have fallen back into old habits. Which meant that he would need someone nearby to trade in the jewelry.

Nikki pushed the door open to the pawn shop and stepped inside. She walked past a collection of baseball cards, piles of sports equipment and an ancient pinball machine. Several glass cases lined the second half of the shop, creating a partition between the shop itself, and the space behind it. Piles of old magazines, RC vehicles, and even a few statues cluttered the space behind the glass cases.

"Hello? Mitch? Are you here?" Nikki paused in front of the center glass case and looked down through the streaked surface at the assortment of jewelry and watches inside.

"Just a second, be right there." A voice drifted out to her through a half-open door. His words were followed by a loud burp. He stepped out through the door, his wild, black curls tangled and heavy as they hung in his face. He was quite a few years older than Nikki. She had been to high school with his brother who was at least ten years younger than him. "Nikki!" He cleared his throat. "You're certainly not who I expected to see."

"Hi Mitch." Nikki smiled at him, and the tiny parakeet perched on his shoulder. "How is Bluebell?"

"Ignoring me as usual." Mitch rolled his eyes. "I must have done something to offend her."

"I'm sure you two will make up soon." Nikki grinned as the bird scuttled to the other side of his shoulder.

"I hope so, but this bird can hold a grudge."

Mitch walked up to the counter. "What can I help you with? A little behind on your rent?"

"No, actually, I'm doing okay." Nikki looked down through the glass again, then back up at him. "I'm actually just here for some information."

"Oh, well that'll cost you." Mitch quirked an eyebrow and rubbed his fingers together. "How much you got?"

"Uh, ten?" Nikki reached into her purse.

"I'm joking!" Mitch burst into loud laughter.

"Oh." Nikki also laughed as she rolled her eyes. "Always such a jokester, Mitch."

"You've gotta be when you're surrounded by riches like this." Mitch gestured to the assortment of dusty items that no one would ever return for. "Now, what kind of information do you need?"

"It's about someone who might have been a customer of yours. A man named Alex." Nikki met his eyes.

"Oh, the cook from the café?" Mitch nodded, then stared hard at her. "You know what happened to him, don't you? Such a tragedy."

"Yes, I know." Nikki frowned. "I'm just curious if he might have been in here recently. Maybe he wanted to pawn something?"

"Sure, he was in here." Mitch rubbed his hand

along his chin. "I'd say just a day or two before he was killed. I can't remember exactly, though. Why do you want to know about him?"

"I'm just trying to find out some information for Gina, she's taking this really hard." Nikki narrowed her eyes as she surveyed the jewelry in the case. "Did he pawn any of this?"

"Oh sure, Gina must be upset. No, he didn't pawn anything. He just came in and asked me a bunch of questions." Mitch shrugged.

"Questions? About what?" Nikki looked up at him.

"Like, how much would I give him for emeralds, for diamonds, those kinds of questions." Mitch pursed his lips. "I never asked him too much about it. I figured he had something to sell, but he never did try to sell it."

"Emeralds and diamonds?" Nikki nodded. "That sounds pretty valuable."

"It can sound that way sure, but really they're not that valuable. Especially if they're hot." Mitch cleared his throat. "I mean, stolen."

"Did you think that was what he had? Stolen jewelry?" Nikki leaned closer to him as he shied back and looked down at the floor.

"He didn't come out and say it, but I figured that

was why he kept asking me questions instead of just showing it to me. It struck me as strange, you know. Plus, I know about him." Mitch lifted an eyebrow. "I knew that he wasn't innocent."

"How do you know about him?" Nikki studied his expression.

"We had never exchanged words, but we had some mutual acquaintances. So, I knew that he had a criminal history. That's why I made it clear to him that I had no interest in dealing in stolen goods." Mitch shook his head. "I've been straight for a long time, and I don't intend to get caught up in that life again."

"And what did he say to that?" Nikki looked into his eyes.

"He said he was going straight, too, and that he didn't want to cause me any trouble." Mitch exhaled and looked up at the ceiling. "Which he didn't. But maybe if I had paid more attention to what he said, maybe I could have figured out what was going on with him. Maybe I could have helped him."

"Maybe." Nikki frowned as she straightened up. "Maybe if I'd seen something or heard one single sound in that alley, I could have stopped him from being killed. There are millions of ways that Alex's death could have been prevented, but it's not your fault." She tilted her head to the side as she watched his face relax. "Do you know if he had any problems, or friendships with anyone in particular, especially while in prison?"

"Not that I heard. I mean, everyone knew that Walter had a big problem with him, but that was it." Mitch picked up a rag and wiped the glass display case, which only led to more smudges.

"Walter?" Nikki's eyes widened. "The Walter that lives here in town? The Walter that has Duke the Boxer?"

"The one and only. Those two had a beef, that's for sure." Mitch tossed the rag back over his shoulder.

"About what?" Nikki prepared to make notes on her phone.

"Can't say." Mitch pursed his lips.

"Can't, or won't?" Nikki met his eyes.

"Can't. I never knew the whole story. At least not for sure. I heard that Walter did time for drug dealing years ago. Rumor is that Walter got picked up for small time drug dealing. He probably would have got a slap on the wrist, but Alex was involved and linked Walter to a much larger drug ring which got Alex out of any charge in return. I think Walter got a much longer sentence because of it. Like I said, I don't know if it was true, it was just rumors I heard. But I did know that it was best to keep the two of them away from each other." Mitch looked up as another customer stepped into the shop. "Can I help you?"

Nikki watched as the two exchanged a few words. She doubted that Mitch had anything else to tell her. But she guessed that Walter did. But would he tell her anything? After their last encounter she doubted it.

As Nikki left the pawn shop she noticed a truck parked in front of Gina's café down the street. She caught a glimpse of Mario walking from the back of it to the front door of the café, with what looked like a very heavy box.

Nikki jogged over and grabbed the door to hold it open for him.

"Thanks." Mario offered a strained smile as he struggled to get the box through the door.

"What are you up to?" Nikki followed him into the café and then to the back room that Gina used for food storage.

"Gina's usual delivery driver refused to drop this order off. I guess he was spooked by the murder. So, I had to go to the next town over, pick it up, and haul it over here." Mario rolled his eyes. "People get so paranoid."

"I can kind of understand his fear." Nikki glanced in the direction of the door that led to the alley. "Something terrible did happen here."

"That's true. But it's over now. Someone settled a score with Alex, and now we all have to move on." Mario set the box down on the floor, then began to shuffle a few of the other boxes piled near the wall.

"You didn't really like Alex working with Gina, did you?" Nikki watched him as he stacked a few of the boxes up.

"No, not really." Mario turned to look at her. "I didn't trust him. She wanted to give him a second chance, but I didn't think it was a good idea."

"Was there some particular reason why you didn't trust him?" Nikki kept her distance as he grabbed another box. She watched the muscles ripple in his arms as he lifted it. He certainly looked strong.

"I had my reasons." Mario grunted as he set the box down on the stack. "I have a lot of work to do." He brushed past her and out the door.

Nikki couldn't shake the feeling that Mario's reasons were quite serious. Why wouldn't he share them?

CHAPTER 12

Nikki wanted to know more about what Mario had against Alex. There were too many mysteries surrounding Alex, and she knew next to nothing about Mario.

Nikki followed Mario out to the truck and picked up one of the lighter boxes.

"So, what exactly didn't you like about him? His criminal history? Or the way he looked at Gina?" Nikki paused as he spun around to face her.

"Excuse me?" Mario locked his eyes to hers.

"You must have seen it." Nikki smiled slightly, the box in her arms serving as a bit of protection from the clear animosity she'd stirred in him. "I saw it, and I only met Alex briefly. He admired her, didn't he? Why wouldn't he? She came to his rescue after all."

"She has too big of a heart." Mario set the box in his arms down and rubbed the back of his neck. "But she's also a little clueless."

Nikki tried not to scowl as his description caused her to bristle. "How so?"

"I told her, he had a thing for her. But she wouldn't believe me. Then one night, he proved it." Mario glanced at her, then quickly away.

"What do you mean?" Nikki tilted her head to the side in an attempt to catch his eyes again. "Mario, how did he prove it?"

"I caught them." Mario winced, then shook his head. "It doesn't matter now. What's done is done."

"You caught them?" Nikki took a sharp breath at the thought of Mario walking in on his girlfriend and Alex having a moment. "So, they were in a relationship?"

"No!" The word burst past Mario's lips with such force that she took a step back.

"Okay, sorry, I had the wrong impression." Nikki stepped back a little farther to create some distance between them. "What happened then?"

"He tried to kiss her, okay?" Mario glared at her. "I don't know why you have to be so nosy about things. None of this matters. Gina set him straight."

"Still, that must have been hard for you to see." Nikki's stomach flipped as she noticed the way he curled his hands into fists. "Alex knew that she was with you, and he still tried to make a move. You didn't confront him about that?"

"Gina took care of it." Mario moved past her, back to the rear of the truck. "I need to get this done. Thanks for your help, but I can take it from here."

Nikki watched as he hauled another box off of the truck. "I'm sorry, Mario, I'm just not buying that you let it go that easily."

"So, it's my job to convince you?" Mario spun around to face her, his handsome features contorted with frustration.

"No, of course not." Nikki took a step back as she read the fury in his eyes. "But I'm willing to bet that you wanted to say a few things to Alex yourself."

"All I wanted was to make sure that he didn't go after Gina again." Mario wiped some sweat from his forehead as he sighed. "Yes, I lost it and punched a few things in anger, but I never touched him. I followed him, just to make sure. But I wasn't going to hurt him. I don't want to go to prison over some fool that doesn't know his boundaries."

"You followed him?" Nikki looked into his eyes. "Where did he go?"

"Every night, the same place. That bar on the corner of Main and Webber. He and Jayden." Mario gestured down the street to the antique store owned by Jayden. His prices were so high that she'd never been able to purchase anything from the shop, but she did like to look through the window at the various items he had on display. It felt a bit like time-traveling to her.

"Maybe if Alex spent less time hanging out with another guy, he could have found a woman that was actually available. I guess you're going to run off and tell your detective boyfriend about this now, right?" Mario slammed his hand against the side of his truck. "I knew if I told the police, they would accuse me of killing him. It doesn't look good, does it?" He looked back at her.

"I won't tell him." Nikki's heart pounded as she wondered if she should. Mario looked good as a suspect. He had motive, evidence of a temper, and he was familiar with Alex's schedule. But even if he was the killer, she didn't want to accuse him, not while he stood there, a few feet away, with no way to protect herself. She guessed that if she pushed him, he might lose his temper. He might confess to how he really felt about Alex. But he might also lose it and hurt her as well. If he was angry enough at Alex for making a move on Gina, to murder him, then it might not take much for him to decide to murder her as well.

Nikki's heart raced as she wondered if her friend was tangled up with a killer. She pulled out her phone as she hurried in the direction of the police station.

Quinn picked up on the first ring. "Nikki? What's up?"

"Do you have a few minutes? I'm right down the street."

"Sure, come by. I literally have about five minutes."

"Okay, I'll be right there." Nikki quickened her pace as she hung up the phone. She knew that Quinn's free time was precious, and he might be using it to have something to eat. As she neared the police station, she was reminded of being there not long before. Her heart skipped a beat. What if the agents were still there? She definitely couldn't go in if they were.

As she was about to turn around and call Quinn

to check, the door swung toward her, and Quinn stepped out. "I thought you might be more comfortable out here."

"Good thinking." Nikki breathed a sigh of relief. "Are our FBI friends still in there?"

"Oh yes, and they're pretty certain that they are running the place now. But they are leaving to interview some people in about an hour. Hopefully, they don't come back." Quinn frowned. "The gun didn't lead anywhere, the serial numbers were shaved off, it can't be traced, it had no fingerprints on it, except for yours. We haven't been able to locate the couple they are tracking. They are pretty good at covering their tracks."

"I hope you can find them soon." Nikki frowned. "I'm sorry to bother you, it's just that I came across some information, and I thought that you might want to have it."

"Wait, are you telling me that almost immediately after you left the police station earlier today, you started digging into the murder again, even though I warned you to stay away from it?" Quinn stared at her.

"Define immediately?" Nikki squinted at him as she anticipated his frustration.

"I should have known that telling you to stay out

of this would be pointless." Quinn shook his head. "How did I ever come across someone as stubborn and brave as you?"

"Maybe you bring it out in me?" Nikki couldn't help but smile.

"What did you find out?" Quinn stopped walking and turned to face her. "Fill me in, before those FBI agents hunt me down."

"I found out that Walter did time. And apparently, he had quite a big problem with Alex." Nikki explained what Mitch had told her. "Did you look into enemies that might have followed Alex home from prison?" She brushed a few muffin crumbs from his suit jacket. "I interrupted your coffee, didn't I?"

"Don't worry about that. I did look into it. I was able to get some of the information that was left out of his file. It looks like he turned in a couple of people in order to secure his release from prison. Unfortunately, I wasn't able to get the names of those he turned in, at least not yet, but I was able to confirm that they are all still behind bars. However, it's still possible that he might have given more information about other criminals. He created a lot of enemies while behind bars." Quinn glanced at his phone as it buzzed. "It looks like my time is up."

"Wait, one more thing." Nikki grabbed his hand. "Gina's boyfriend, Mario. Do you know if he has a criminal history?"

"I don't believe so." Quinn frowned. "Why?"

"He caught Alex trying to kiss Gina. He seems like the jealous type." Nikki lowered her voice as she decided not to tell Quinn everything just yet. She didn't want to upset Gina and get Mario into trouble if he was innocent. "I know Gina would be pretty upset if she knew I asked, but to be honest, I'm a little worried about her dating him, if it's possible that he killed Alex."

"I'll dig a little deeper and see what I can find." Quinn met her eyes. "I have to go, I'm sorry."

"Don't be sorry." Nikki shook her head. "You need to get back to work."

"Thanks for the tips." Quinn kissed her once more, then started to walk away.

Nikki smiled as she watched him walk back to the police station. She pulled out her phone and sent a quick text to Sonia, then she started down the sidewalk.

CHAPTER 13

As Nikki neared the café again, she heard the roar of an engine. Mario's truck peeled away from the curb and tore down the street.

Nikki wondered if she might have spooked him. As she waited for Sonia's response to her text, she noticed Gina's car pull up to the café. She started to raise her hand to wave to her but changed her mind. How could she speak to her at the moment, when she knew that Gina hadn't told her about what Alex had done? She needed to work out how to broach the subject with her.

"Nikki?" Sonia walked up to her with Princess at her side. "Didn't you see Gina there?"

"I did." Nikki tucked her phone back into her pocket. "I didn't expect you to come right away."

"It seemed like the best thing to do. You're right, the crime scene might still have something to tell us." Sonia tipped her head toward the café. "Should we let Gina know what we're up to?"

"No, I think she needs some time alone." Nikki filled Sonia in on her encounter with Mario as they walked across the street to Woof Way.

"Is everything okay between the two of you?" Sonia looked over at her as they reached the end of the alley.

"I hope so." Nikki took a deep breath, then sighed. "She seems very protective of Mario. I don't want to upset her. I just wish this never happened."

"Me too. But we can't change the past, we can only work on finding out the truth about what happened." Sonia nodded as she glanced over at her.

"I just keep wishing that I had seen something, heard something, sensed something." Nikki looked down the empty alley. "If I had, then maybe I could have prevented all of this."

"Nikki." Sonia followed her gaze. "There was nothing that you could have done. The killer must have known that the sound would be drowned out. You didn't see or hear anything, because the killer didn't want you to see or hear anything."

"But that's the key, isn't it?" Nikki turned to face her. "How does someone pull off a murder without being seen or heard? The killer had to know the alley well. Someone had access to it. Easy access. Quick access. They had a way in, and they knew the way out." Nikki stood at the end of the alley and stared down it. "The only ways to access the alley, aside from walking around the front, is through the backyards that back on to the path behind the shops, or the delivery doors of the shops. I mean that's how Alex accessed it, through the door that led out from the café's kitchen. The apartments above the shops on the other side of Woof Way aren't in use. They have been sold and are going to be converted into offices next year. They had to get into the alley through the back because they didn't walk past Gina and me sitting at the table out front."

"Since you found the gun not far from the end of the alley, I would guess that was the way the killer came and went." Sonia pointed to the end of the alley. "Through the garden where you found the gun."

"Yes, you're probably right." Nikki squinted in the direction of the end of the alley. "But how does someone crawl through all of that without being seen?"

"I don't know." Sonia sighed as she looked over the brush. "I guess it's possible, though."

"I want to have a closer look." Nikki started toward the tangled brush. As she did, the side door to the café swung open.

Nikki spun around to see Tyler, Gina's busboy, step into the alley.

"You startled me!" Nikki frowned as she walked over to him.

"I startled you?" Tyler chuckled. "I'm where I'm supposed to be, what are you two doing here?"

"Just walking Princess." Sonia scooped up the small dog. "Nikki, we're going to take a stroll out front."

"Alright, I'll be right there." Nikki nodded to her, then turned her attention back to Tyler. "The café is closed, why are you here?"

"I'm just trying to get things back in order for Gina." Tyler shrugged. "It upsets her to talk about it. So, I've just been trying to focus on the job."

"It must upset you, too." Nikki met his eyes as he pulled a pack of cigarettes from his pocket.

"Sure, it's pretty scary. Just to think that he was here one day, and the next, he's gone." Tyler popped the cigarette between his lips, then offered the pack to her.

"No, thank you." Nikki frowned as he flicked on a lighter. "Did you get to know Alex pretty well? I'm sure that you two worked together a lot."

"Not exactly. He just saw me as the grunt, he'd bark orders at me. We didn't exactly become friends." Tyler glanced back at the door of the café, stared at it for a moment, then looked back at Nikki. "Don't tell Gina I told you this, but I didn't really like the guy."

"You didn't?" Nikki's eyes narrowed. "Was there any reason why? Did he do anything to upset you?"

"I just didn't trust him. Gina took a big chance on him, but I didn't think that he deserved it, really. He just seemed sketchy. A few times these people came in asking about him, and he'd make me lie to them and tell them I'd never heard of him." Tyler rolled his eyes. "Any time someone doesn't want to be found, that's a pretty good sign that they're up to something."

"True." Nikki offered a small smile as she wondered if the people he mentioned were the same ones that the FBI had been tracking. "Do you know who these people were?"

"Just some couple, a husband and wife, or boyfriend and girlfriend, I'm not sure. I just know the way they talked to each other made it seem like they were together." Tyler flicked some ash from his cigarette. "I guess he didn't want to talk to them because he got pretty mad whenever I told him they were here to see him."

Nikki asked him to describe them. From the description she guessed it was possible they were the Hales.

"Did they come in often?" Nikki pulled her phone out of her pocket and made a note about the couple on it.

"Two or three times in the last week or so." Tyler pursed his lips. "I don't know, I didn't exactly keep track."

"I understand." Nikki looked up at him. "What about any other visitors? Did he make any friends around town that you know of?"

"Not really. He would hang out in the alley with Jayden sometimes. Most days when Alex took out the trash, he would chat with Jayden." Tyler shook his head. "I have no idea what they had to talk about, but whenever I stepped out here, those two would go quiet, like they'd just been telling secrets." He curled his upper lip. "Like I would want to know what they were talking about, anyway."

"There must have been something that Alex did

that made you more suspicious." Nikki leaned against the wall beside him and did her best to ignore the smoke that curled around her face. "You can tell me."

"He wasn't responsible. And, he lied to Gina." Tyler took another long drag.

"About what?" Nikki turned to face him.

"Alex lost the key for the shed." Tyler blew a stream of smoke from between his lips. "He was worried that he was going to get fired for losing it. I told him he should just tell Gina, and she would get him a new copy. But he wouldn't. So, I told him there's another key on Gina's key ring." He shrugged as he took another drag of his cigarette.

"Do you think he took those keys?" Nikki shifted away from the next stream of smoke he released.

"I think he had to get in the shed somehow. I don't know if he took them or not. But if he didn't tell Gina, then he probably did. Maybe he thought he could get a new copy made before she noticed. I've got to get back in there." Tyler tossed his cigarette on the ground and crushed the burning end with his shoe.

Nikki considered his words as she walked out to

the front of the shop. If Alex had taken Gina's keys, that would explain why they were missing. But why weren't they found in his pocket?

CHAPTER 14

Nikki spotted Sonia and Princess near the end of the alley and walked over to them. She knelt down to stroke Princess' head. Princess jumped on Nikki's legs with excitement.

"Hi, baby." Nikki smiled as she rubbed behind Princess' ears.

"Anything?" Sonia looked at her with a hopeful gleam in her eyes.

"Not much." Nikki sighed. "Only that Alex probably stole Gina's keys. They weren't missing after all. But now they are, because they weren't in Alex's pocket when he was examined."

"So, if he had them in his pocket when he was killed, that means that the killer might have taken them out of his pocket." Sonia kept Princess close to her side as she followed Nikki back toward the alley. "But why? To go after Gina?"

"It's possible, but I don't think so." Nikki paused at the end of the alley and pointed out the shed positioned beside the café. "I think someone wants to get in that shed." She stared at the small structure. "But why?"

"To steal things?" Sonia peered at the shed, then frowned. "What could be of value that's stored in it?"

"Spare kitchen equipment? Cleaning supplies?" Nikki shook her head as she walked toward the shed. "None of that would motivate someone to kill, would it?"

"So, you think that someone killed Alex for the keys in his pocket?" Sonia narrowed her eyes as she followed after Nikki. "But how would the killer know that he had the keys on him?"

"I'm not sure. But if the killer took the keys, then my guess is he or she will be back here to get what they were looking for. I've already asked Quinn to keep an eye on Gina's house, since her house keys were on that key ring, too. I think she's arranging for the locks to be replaced. But I think we need to keep an eye on this shed, too."

"Have you asked Gina about it?" Sonia squinted

at the door of the shed. "Did she put a new lock on it?"

"I don't know. With the keys being missing, she might have, but I'm not sure." Nikki tried the lock on the door of the shed. She gave it a hard tug, but it refused to open.

"You should ask her about that, and also about what might be in this shed." Sonia turned to look at her. "Nikki, I know she's your friend, she's my friend, too. But let's be honest about what's happened here. She hired an ex-con, and her keys were stolen. Then that employee was murdered, maybe for the keys to this shed."

"You think she might be involved?" Nikki took a sharp breath. "You think maybe Alex had the stolen jewelry in the shed and she knew about it? Or she might be storing something illegal in the shed?"

"I think it's possible, and I think that if we tell Quinn our suspicions, we might be getting Gina into more trouble than we'd like." Sonia looked back at the café. "Let's see if she'll tell us the truth."

"You're right." Nikki started toward the café, then paused. "Let me talk to her alone first. She might be more willing to tell the truth, if she doesn't feel surrounded."

"That's fine. I want to talk to Jayden, anyway.

See if he saw or he knows anything." Sonia looked toward the antique store. "But be careful, Nikki. You and Gina are friends, but desperate people do desperate things." She steered Princess toward the store.

"I will be." Nikki sighed as she walked around to the front of the café. She wasn't so sure that Gina would still be her friend after she asked her the questions that floated through her mind.

Nikki knocked lightly on the locked front door of the café.

Moments later Gina unlocked the door and opened it. "Nikki, it's good to see you." She smiled as she waved her inside.

"You too." Nikki gave her a quick hug. "How are you holding up?"

"I've been better." Gina cringed, then shrugged. "But we have to move on, right?"

"Right." Nikki cleared her throat. "Did you ever find your keys?"

"No. Not yet. I don't know where I put them." Gina shook her head. "With all that's going on, I may never find them."

"What if you didn't lose them?" Nikki met her eyes. "What if someone took them?"

"Why?" Gina frowned.

"You tell me. Is there anything in the shed that someone would kill over?" Nikki stood up straight.

"Excuse me?" Gina pursed her lips. "Are you asking what I think you're asking?"

"I'm just asking whether someone would want to get to something valuable that might be in the shed?" Nikki held up her hands. "Gina, I'm not interested in causing you any trouble, but if there's something more going on here, you need to tell me, so that I can help you."

"It doesn't feel much like a question." Gina crossed her arms as she stared at Nikki. "It feels more like an accusation to me."

"It's not." Nikki touched her forearm and frowned. "I just want to know if you're in danger."

"If I am, it's not because of anything I've done." Gina pulled away from her touch.

"I'm sorry, Gina." Nikki sighed as she took a step back. "I didn't mean to upset you."

"Actually." Gina looked up at her, her eyes widened. "Yes, we did have a break-in a few days ago." She took a sip of her drink, then shook her head. "No actually, it wasn't technically a break-in, because the lock wasn't broken. But the entire shed was ripped apart, stuff thrown everywhere. It was as if someone was looking for something."

"What was taken?" Nikki met Gina's eyes.

"Nothing. Nothing that I could pinpoint. It was such a mess that it was hard to say at first, but I cleaned it all up, and as far as I could tell everything was accounted for." Gina winced as she shook her head. "Alex had left the door unlocked."

"He did? How do you know that?"

"He had to have left it unlocked. He went in after Tyler had left for the day and Alex and I were the only ones with access to the key. The lock wasn't broken." Gina bit into her bottom lip. "He tried to deny it of course. He was probably afraid that I was going to fire him. I told him that I just wanted to know the truth, and I think he was about to tell me the truth, but before he could, Jayden from next door interrupted him. He insisted that he saw Alex lock the shed."

"And what did you think when he said that? Did you believe him?" Nikki pulled out her phone and began to make a few notes on it.

"I had no reason not to believe him, other than the fact that he's completely untrustworthy. Everyone knows that Jayden isn't an honest person. He bends the rules about everything." Gina rolled her eyes. "He thinks he can get away with anything."

"Gina, tell me the truth about Alex. I know that you and Alex had a moment." Nikki stared into her eyes. "You told me that you weren't together."

"We weren't." Gina glared at Nikki and crossed her arms. "I am with Mario. I thought I made that clear?"

"But according to Mario, something did happen between you and Alex." Nikki did her best not to see Gina as her friend. She wanted to be as impartial as possible. But she also didn't want to upset her. As much as she didn't want to believe that Gina might have been involved in a crime that led to the death of a man who just had the opportunity to start a new life, she couldn't ignore the fact that she might have been involved in his murder.

"Did Mario tell you that?" Gina bit into her bottom lip, then shook her head. "I cared about Alex, that much is true." She sighed. "I thought he could really turn things around for himself. I believed in him. That's why I took a chance on him. Then one afternoon when we were closing up, we were talking about his future. He started telling me how grateful he was that I'd hired him and been so supportive of him. One thing led to another, and all of a sudden he was trying to kiss me. I didn't let him." She looked back at Nikki. "I stopped him. We were both embarrassed. I guess he wasn't used to someone doing something for him that he misread my intentions. When I made it clear that I had no interest in him and that I was with Mario, he was very apologetic. I think he got scared that I was going to fire him. But I understood it was just a mistake." She cringed. "Unfortunately, Mario was not so understanding. He was furious."

"Did he threaten to hurt Alex?" Nikki met her eyes.

"No, he would never do that." Gina shook her head. "I think I need a break from all of this. I think it's time for you to leave." She pointed to the door.

"Of course." Nikki nodded. "I'm just trying to help."

"I know, but it sure doesn't feel that way to me at the moment. I really need a break from all of this." Gina pointed to the door again, then turned and walked away.

Nikki stepped out of the café, her chest tight with dread. Had she made a mistake by pushing Gina too hard? It seemed to her that her friend didn't know anything about the possibility of her boyfriend killing Alex, but she could be hiding it. She looked up to see Sonia and Princess walking toward her.

CHAPTER 15

"How did it go?" Nikki smiled at Sonia as she patted Princess' head.

"After I spoke to Jayden at the antique store, I ordered a sandwich from the bakery down the street. It was a good excuse to talk to Josh and Adam, the owners. I wanted to see if they had seen anything yesterday that might help, but they hadn't." Sonia met her near the door of the café. "Maybe you could offer it to Quinn and see where he's at with the case?"

"Great idea." Nikki recounted her conversation with Gina to Sonia. "I'm afraid I'm not going to get much more out of her. I may have permanently burned that bridge."

"I'm sorry, Nikki." Sonia looked at her. "I know

you don't want to believe that Gina could have anything to do with this."

"No, I don't." Nikki sighed. "I just hope she didn't. Maybe Quinn will be able to clear some things up. Are you okay with Princess? Do you want me to take her with me?" She reached for the leash.

"No, don't worry about us, we'll be just fine. We'll see you later for her walk. I just feel like snuggling with her for a bit. The sooner this is solved the better." Sonia glanced at her watch. "I should get back, though, she's overdue for her meal. Keep me up to date on what you find out, alright?"

"Sure, I will." Nikki started to turn away, then paused. "Did Jayden mention anything interesting?"

"No, we didn't have much of a chance to talk. He had some other customers. A couple. A little strange, if you ask me. They seemed to be waiting for me to leave before they spoke to Jayden. Maybe I was just imagining it, though." Sonia led Princess toward her car.

With the thought of Gina's annoyance at her weighing on her mind, Nikki walked in the direction of the police station. It felt as if she'd been walking in circles all day. Each new bit of information she discovered sent her mind spinning. Nothing was adding up, at least not enough to provide a clear and unquestionable suspect. She hoped that Quinn had better luck.

As Nikki paused outside the police station, she wondered if she could really go through with walking inside. The memory of handcuffs around her wrists still caused her muscles to tighten. But she couldn't let fear prevent her from trying to get to the truth, or from seeing Quinn. He had texted to let her know the coast was clear, the FBI agents had left for the day, but her heart still raced at the thought of entering the station. After taking a deep breath she pulled the door open and stepped inside.

Business carried on inside the lobby of the police station. She walked past the front desk with only a brief nod from the officer behind it. He barely looked in her direction. Was her walk of shame already forgotten?

As Nikki neared Quinn's office, she braced herself for his reaction. Would he be bothered that she wanted to interrupt him yet again?

"Quinn?" Nikki knocked lightly on the frame of his open office door.

"Look at you." Quinn sighed as he smiled at her. "A sight for sore eyes, that's for sure."

"Thanks." Nikki smiled in return as she stepped through the door. "I know you're busy but—"

"But you want to pick my brain?" Quinn gestured to the chair in front of his desk. "You know you're always welcome."

"I brought you a sandwich from the bakery. Actually, Sonia asked me to make sure that it got to you." Nikki held out the white paper bag and smiled at his wide eyes. "Hungry?"

"So hungry." Quinn grabbed the bag. "Remind me to kiss Mrs. Whitter the next time I see her."

"And what about the delivery girl?" Nikki leaned close and puckered her lips.

"I guess I do owe you a tip." Quinn chuckled. "But the kiss will have to wait." He glanced around the station at the bustle of officers.

"Of course. I just hope that's not how you tip all of your delivery girls." Nikki settled in the chair across from him.

"I would never." Quinn winked at her. "Thanks, I really needed an energy boost."

"Still struggling to find a lead?" Nikki met his eyes.

"I'm working on it but nothing is really panning out." Quinn unwrapped his sandwich.

"What about Walter?" Nikki asked.

"Nothing more than what you told me." Quinn took a bite of his sandwich.

"Presuming what I heard is true, if Walter got a longer sentence because of Alex, it might be enough for him to hold a grudge, don't you think?" Nikki met his eyes.

"Whatever happened was years ago. It sounds like Alex was just a dumb kid trying to keep himself out of prison and maybe make a name for himself, the wrong way. Why would Walter kill him now?" Quinn shook his head. "It doesn't make sense to me."

"Maybe it doesn't have to." Nikki shrugged as she sat back in her chair. "Walter's life changed that day. Prison changes people. He could have gone on to have a different life, if he hadn't ever been convicted of such a serious crime. I'd say that kind of anger could certainly fester over the years."

"It's possible." Quinn nodded. "I haven't ruled it out. It's just that it seems so unlikely to me. Walter committed a low key crime and did his time, and since then has gone on to live a pretty clean life. To make a leap from that to murder is a huge change."

"But it's possible." Nikki tried to imagine what it must have been like for Walter to see Alex again. Had he recognized him right away? Had it sat in the back of his mind until he finally put two and two together? "I found out some more interesting things today." She began to fill him in on her discussions with Mario, and Gina. "Did you know that the shed at the café was broken into a few days ago?"

"No." Quinn frowned. "I don't think Gina filed a report."

"I guess that makes sense, since nothing was taken and nothing of real value is stored in there." Nikki shrugged.

"But you think differently?" Quinn smiled, which immediately made Nikki relax.

"I'm not sure. I do think there was something in that shed that someone was after, though." Nikki tapped her finger against his desk. "I'm just not sure what it is."

"Let's run through what we do know." Quinn leaned back in his chair. "We know that Alex had a bad history. We know that at least one couple, the Hales, were looking for him because of the jewelry that they thought he had. We know that he made a pass at Gina, and that Mario knew about it. We also know that he has a history with Walter, and any number of other people that he did time with."

Nikki was surprised he was prepared to discuss the case so openly with her.

Quinn slid out a photo array and placed it in front of Nikki.

"These are all of the people I've been able to track down so far that I know he gave information about. We've shown them to Gina and the other people that live and work near the café, but they all said they haven't seen any of them." Quinn pointed at the photos. "Have you seen any of them?"

"I haven't seen any of them." Nikki looked over each of the faces in the array. "Wow, he was quite busy making enemies, wasn't he?"

"It's a tough thing to turn against others, it put him in real danger. But it's also a pretty good sign that he actually was trying to turn his life around."

"It is, or it would be, if it were true." Nikki leaned forward. "But what if that's not the case?"

"What do you mean?" Quinn narrowed his eyes.

"What if Alex wasn't trying to turn his life around? What if he used his time in jail to go after people he considered to be enemies? And what if he did have that stolen jewelry? Maybe he kept it in the shed. Maybe that's why it was broken into." Nikki raised her eyebrows. "He could have been playing everyone the entire time."

"That's true." Quinn ran his hand down the length of his chin. "If he was, then he may have double crossed the wrong person. If only we could locate the Hales, we could try and find out more about what they might know."

"I hope you can." Nikki gestured to the sandwich. "Make sure you eat. I have to pick up the dogs for their walks."

"Tell Spots hi for me." Quinn met her eyes as she paused near the door. "Maybe we can try and have a nice, quiet dinner, if I have time tonight."

"Sounds good. I know you're very busy. I'll make sure Spots gets lots of attention." Nikki smiled as she left his office.

As Nikki left the police station her mind swirled with everything she had learned about Alex and his past. She needed her walk with the dogs more than ever to sort through the day.

CHAPTER 16

Nikki headed for Sesame's house first. The small dog had a lot of energy and required quite a bit of exercise. She braced herself for Julie's reaction to seeing her. Their last encounter hadn't been great, and now that she knew so much more about Alex, she could understand Julie's problem with Sesame being around him at the café, presuming that's why she didn't want Sesame going there. But she had no idea how Julie would know about his past. Rumors? As she approached the front door, she saw Julie on the front step with Sesame beside her.

"Hi Julie." Nikki smiled as she scooped Sesame up into her arms. "I've been looking forward to seeing this little girl."

"She's been looking forward to seeing you, too." Julie smiled as she trailed her hand through the Toy Poodle's soft fur. "I wish I could take her on these walks myself, but I don't think she would have nearly as much fun without you."

"Oh, I'm sure she'd love to walk with you." Nikki set Sesame down on the ground and wrapped her leash around her wrist. "Would you like to join us?"

"Oh, I can't walk too far." Julie tapped her hand against her chest. "I get so winded."

"That's alright. You can just join us for a short loop, and then we can continue on with our walk after. What do you think?" Nikki looked into her eyes. A walk would be a great way to try to get a little information out of Julie.

"Okay, just a short loop, though." Julie smiled as she stepped out through the door. "It's been so long since I enjoyed one. With my breathing, it just makes it nearly impossible to do physical things."

"We'll take it nice and slow." Nikki started out at a casual pace. "Is it asthma you're dealing with?"

"No, it's far more than that. I'm afraid I have heart failure." Julie sighed, then shook her head. "Don't worry, I'm not going to die on you. I'm on medication for it, and I actually may survive quite some time with it. But little things just wear me out so easily. I have to be careful."

"Absolutely." Nikki frowned as she studied her. "Do you have anyone to help you? Family?"

"No family I'm afraid. It was just me and my dad for a long time, and then he passed away. So, now it's just me." Julie shrugged as she looked down the sidewalk ahead of her. "I never expected this, you know? I never expected to be so alone. I mean I have Sesame, but I miss my dad."

Nikki put her hand on Julie's shoulder. She was surprised at how weak Julie appeared compared to their last encounter.

"You're not alone, I'm here."

"And I'm so glad you are." Julie flashed her a smile. "I see now, what Sonia sees in you. When she mentioned you were her dog walker, and her best friend, I thought she was losing it a bit. How can a woman of her age be best friends with someone as young as you?" She laughed. "But I get it now."

"Sonia is an amazing friend." Nikki smiled at the thought of Sonia's recommendation. "I have learned a lot from her."

"And she has learned a lot from you, I imagine."

Julie sighed as she slowed her pace even further. "Sometimes I wonder what it would be like to have that kind of connection to someone. I thought once I would have a husband, children, but it never worked out. I was so heartbroken after my father died, I just couldn't connect with people."

"I'm so sorry about your father. That must have been so devastating for you." Nikki watched as Sesame stuck her nose into a flower that a bee had its eye on as well.

"It's funny how people say that." Julie frowned. "That it was devastating. As if it somehow stays in the past. For me, it still is. I guess that's the danger of having such a close relationship with someone. When they're gone, it's like your whole life is gone, too."

"He must have been a wonderful man." Nikki steered Sesame away from the bee, while contemplating Julie's words. "What was he like?"

"He was wonderful. But also, terrible." Julie grinned and rolled her eyes. "He had this way of getting himself into trouble that drove me insane. He always wanted the best for me. He would do anything to make sure that I had everything he thought I should have. Unfortunately, that led him down some paths he never should have set foot on."

She held out her phone. "This is him." She smiled. "Not long before he died."

"Like what kind of paths?" Nikki held her breath as she hoped that Julie would share more. As she gazed at the picture on the screen, her heart skipped a beat. There was no question in her mind that Julie's father was one of the men in the photo array that Quinn had showed her of people that Alex had double crossed.

"Like, making some business deals that weren't exactly legal. Like, trusting the wrong people." Julie narrowed her eyes. Her body tensed, and her voice grew harder. "I tried to warn him. But he wouldn't listen to me. He was a bit sexist you know, and he didn't think his daughter could have a valid opinion when it came to money and business."

"That didn't frustrate you?" Nikki raised an eyebrow.

"Not really. Those were the times, you know? He didn't know any better. I tried to get him to listen to me, but he refused. He paid the price for it. He almost finished a prison sentence, when someone turned him in for another crime to save his own skin. His sentence was extended, and not even a month later he had a heart attack." Julie stopped in the middle of the sidewalk and drew a shaky breath. "I'm sorry, I think this is a bit too much for me."

"It's alright." Nikki put her hand gently on her elbow and looked into her eyes. "Rest as long as you need, then we can head back."

"Thank you." Julie patted her chest. "This ticker, it just doesn't want to make the effort anymore."

"I hope the medicine will help." Nikki nodded. It had been a productive walk. Julie certainly had plenty of motive to want to kill Alex. Of course, whether she could have been the murderer was dependent on two things. Julie had to know that Alex was the reason her father's sentence had been increased, which it appeared she did. That's probably why she didn't want Sesame going to Gina's café, but did she have the strength to be able to kill him? She couldn't walk a full block. She could easily be overcome. How could she walk into the alley and leave undetected?

"Okay, I'm ready I think." Julie turned back toward the house. "You two go on, I can make it back on my own."

"I'd rather walk with you, if that's okay." Nikki matched her pace to Julie's. "I've really enjoyed talking with you."

"Oh, you're sweet." Julie smiled, then waved her hand. "I'm sure you'd much rather be talking with your boyfriend. Quinn, right?"

"Yes." Nikki glanced over at her. "Do you know him?"

"We've chatted." Julie nodded and then lowered her voice. "Plus, the rumor mill around here never slows down. Everyone is taking bets on when the two of you are going to get married."

"Married? Already?" Nikki laughed. "I don't think we're quite ready for that."

"Well, don't wait too long. Take it from me." Julie patted Nikki's shoulder. "It may seem like you have all the time in the world, but one day you will open your eyes, and wonder where the time went."

Nikki paused at the end of the walkway that led up to Julie's house.

"That's good advice, Julie, thank you."

"Take it." Julie winked at her. "Before it's too late."

Nikki followed her up to the front door. "Let me get you some water." She stepped through the door behind her.

"I can manage, it's alright, I just need one of my pills." Julie sank down into an overstuffed easy chair and closed her eyes.

"Here." Nikki picked up the glass of water on the table beside Julie's chair and offered it to her. As she did, she noticed the bottle of pills on the table as well. She tried to see the label to see the name of the medicine as Julie picked up the bottle and opened it up, but she couldn't see it. When she set the bottle back down, Nikki noticed a tremble in her hand.

"Are you sure you're okay? Do you want me to call an ambulance?" Nikki frowned.

"I'm fine, I promise." Julie waved her hand. "Sesame needs her walk. I'll be here when you get back." She winked at her. "Go on, now, I need a little rest."

Nikki hesitated. She hated to leave the clearly ill woman there alone, but she also knew what it was like to want her privacy when she didn't feel well. She quietly stepped out of the house, then she guided Sesame down the sidewalk once more.

Nikki headed in the direction of Sonia's house. A good walk might just help her sort through everything. When she neared the house, Sesame yelped and jumped into the air.

"Oh, excited to see Princess, are you?" Nikki smiled down at her. No matter how much she had on her mind, the boundless joy that dogs exuded always managed to bring a smile back to her lips.

"There you are." Sonia stepped outside with Princess in her arms. "We were hoping to see you soon."

"Sorry for the delay." Nikki laughed as Princess squirmed out of Sonia's grasp, eager to greet Sesame. "These two are like best friends these days."

"That's great." Sonia smiled as she handed over the leash. "What did Quinn have to say?"

"Oh, I have so much to tell you." Nikki started down the driveway with the two dogs running ahead of her. Their leashes at full stretch. "I spoke with Julie about her father, and it turns out that he was in prison, and died in prison, due to someone ratting on him. Three guesses who?"

"Alex?" Sonia's eyes widened.

"I believe so. I'm not sure if Julie knows it was Alex or not, but I suspect that she must, after she reacted the way she did when I took Sesame to the café. So, presuming she does, then we have ourselves a new suspect." Nikki shook her head. "I just don't see her committing the murder, though, she seems so weak. How did she kill Alex undetected? She isn't exactly quick on her feet. I doubt that she would have the strength to commit the murder."

"Let me be the judge of that." Sonia pursed her lips as she looked at Nikki.

"What do you mean? She's in heart failure, she barely made it around the block." Nikki lifted an eyebrow.

"So she says. But I've heard some rumors about her. Rumors that I'm going to check up on. You finish your walk, I'll be waiting for you when you get back." Sonia turned and walked back toward the house.

Nikki continued on with the dogs and picked up the rest of them as she passed their houses. Coco had his nose in everything, from the trash cans that weren't yet pulled back from the curb to the rabbit holes they passed.

"Easy, pup." She sighed as she pulled him back again.

Spots gave a stern bark and nudged Coco with his lean frame.

"No fighting." Nikki reached down to pet them. As she rounded back through the neighborhood and dropped off each of the dogs, she noticed how quiet everything was. No one stood on their porches waiting to share a conversation with a neighbor. No one shouted for their children to come in. The town was still nervous. After she dropped off Sesame, and checked to be sure that Julie was okay, she walked back to Sonia's house.

"What do you think, Princess? Could Julie be a killer?" Nikki scrunched up her nose at the thought. She still couldn't picture it.

CHAPTER 17

Sonia greeted Nikki and Princess at the door with a notebook in one hand, and a glass of iced tea in the other. She gave Nikki the tea and picked up Princess in her free hand for a cuddle. Princess licked her cheeks.

"I've done my research." Sonia led Nikki to the dining room table. "Those rumors I told you about, are that Julie is playing a con game. She's not actually sick."

"That doesn't seem possible." Nikki sat down at the table and took a sip of the iced tea.

"It doesn't, but that is the rumor. Apparently, the theory is that she's faking her illness to gain sympathy and attention. She certainly isn't doing it for money." Sonia sat down across from her. Princess nestled in her lap.

"I saw her medication on the table." Nikki smiled as Princess glanced between them. "I couldn't see what it was, but she had some of the medication and said it was for her heart failure."

"Maybe, but maybe she just has the medicine bottle, and fills it with candy." Sonia put Princess in her dog bed beside the table. She curled into a ball and lay down. "Unfortunately, I can't prove whether she's faking it. But I do think we need to consider that it's a possibility."

"Another possibility. I feel like all we have are possibilities." Nikki had a sip of her tea. "How are we supposed to narrow them down when Alex had so many enemies?"

"We have to start from what we know." Sonia splayed her hands across the table. "What is something we are certain about?"

"It had to be someone that knew his routine." Nikki nodded as she took a breath. "Think about it. Whoever killed him likely knew that he would come out of the café to put the trash out shortly after closing every day."

"But didn't Tyler say that most days Jayden would

go out at the same time to chat with him? So, he usually would have been with someone. Surely the killer would have known that." Sonia tapped her pencil on the piece of paper in front of her and reviewed the list she'd created. "We know that Alex had a few enemies and really only one friend in town aside from Gina. So, if we want to look for someone who knew his routine, that only leaves us a few options."

"That's true. Tyler said that Jayden would often meet Alex in the alley. But he wasn't in the alley the day that Alex was killed." Nikki narrowed her eyes. "On the day Alex needed Jayden the most, he happened to not be in the alley?"

"As you said, if the killer knew Alex's routine, then the killer would have known that Alex would be in the alley at that time, and Jayden would often be there as well. Maybe the killer did something to distract Jayden, so that there would be time for the murder to happen, without the killer being caught." Sonia quirked an eyebrow. "Of course, that would mean that this is less a crime of passion and more a premeditated murder. Someone didn't just wake up one day and decide to kill him. Someone decided to carry out this murder, and planned it out, maybe even for weeks, but at least for more than a day."

Sonia's words lifted a fog from Nikki's thoughts.

She hadn't considered the planning. She hadn't thought about how much effort went into this murder.

"You're absolutely right." Nikki sank down into a chair and closed her eyes. "How did I miss that? That means that whoever did this was not only aware of Alex's routine, but also knew enough about Jayden to distract him. Wow, what if this is a partner situation?"

"There is that couple, the Hales, they were after the stolen jewelry. Could one of them have been in the alley and the other distracting Jayden?" Sonia snapped her fingers. "I bet that's it. They made sure he would be alone in the alley and then the one who didn't commit the murder made sure that the coast was clear for their partner. It makes perfect sense."

"Yes, it does." Nikki frowned as she stood up from her chair. "There's only one problem."

"What problem?" Sonia met her eyes.

"We have no way to prove it. We can say it makes sense, but we have no physical evidence to connect them to the murder, we have no eyewitness to place them at the scene of the crime. We don't even know where they are, as far as I know the police haven't been able to find them. Figuring out what happened doesn't equal proving it."

"You're right." Sonia winced. "But wait." She looked up at Nikki again. "If you tell Quinn about it, he might be able to come up with something that would prove it. At least he can look deeper into it to find out if we're right."

"Yes, he could. But if I bother him with this now, with no proof, I feel like I'm only going to be distracting him. He's already in trouble for standing up for me when I was taken in for questioning. I really don't want to cause him any more trouble at work." Nikki bit into her bottom lip as she considered her options. "I think the best thing to do is get the proof first."

"Sure, that would be great." Sonia stood up from the table. "But how are you going to do that? The gun couldn't be traced, it was clean, except for your fingerprints. There's nothing in the alley to connect the Hales, like you said. What are you going to find?"

"Maybe an eyewitness." Nikki crossed her arms. "If I can get Jayden to admit that he was distracted by the husband and wife team, then maybe that will be enough to get a warrant for their arrest. Or maybe, he saw more than he's admitting to."

"If he did, then why wouldn't he say something about it? Alex was his friend. I would think he would want the murderer caught." Sonia narrowed her eyes. "Don't you think so?"

"Sure, I think so. But there are people who will do anything to avoid talking to the police. Maybe Jayden has something to hide. Maybe he doesn't want to be questioned. Maybe he was embarrassed. Maybe he didn't want to admit he had been distracted and Alex had been killed because of it. Or maybe he's scared. Maybe he was threatened by whoever distracted him, that if he said anything, he would be next to be killed. We have to figure out what really happened, and that means digging a little deeper." Nikki met Sonia's eyes. "What do you say?"

"I say, I'll get my purse." Sonia grinned as she hurried over to the hook it hung on. Princess jumped out of her bed and followed after Sonia. "Let's find out the truth."

"I think we should use the same tactic." Nikki held open the front door for her. "One of us can distract Jayden, while the other takes a look around the store. If there's something there that can prove the couple's involvement in all of this, it's the evidence that we can give Quinn that maybe he can use to get an arrest warrant." A faint buzz carried through Nikki's nerves as she closed the door behind them. "We're so close, Sonia, I can feel it."

"Me too." Sonia hurried to the car, with Princess at her side. "But let's make sure we're careful about it. If we spook Jayden, he might never tell the truth about any of it."

"Very careful." Nikki nodded as she climbed into the passenger seat of Sonia's car.

Princess jumped up into her lap and curled up. Nikki ran her hand along the dog's back.

On the drive to the antique store, Nikki's heart began to race. This was it. She was certain that this would be the clue that revealed what really happened to Alex in the alley.

"Good, he's still open." Sonia tipped her head toward the open sign in the front window of the antique store. "You distract him, I'll take a look around."

"Are you sure?" Nikki frowned as she stepped out of the car.

"Absolutely. I have Princess to use as an excuse. Just trust me." Sonia winked at Nikki as she scooped the little dog up into her arms and headed for the entrance of the antique store.

Nikki admired Sonia's bravery. At times she wondered how the petite woman could be so bold.

Nikki had a hard time asserting herself, but Sonia had been teaching her well since their friendship blossomed. Sonia knew how to go after exactly what she wanted, without any hesitation. Nikki just hoped they weren't walking straight toward danger.

CHAPTER 18

As Nikki watched Sonia head for the door of the antique store and swing it open, Nikki almost called her back. Was Jayden somehow involved in the murder? Had they missed something?

"Sonia! Wait for me!" Nikki hurried to catch up with her.

Sonia held the door open for her and met her eyes. "Deep breath, Nikki, we've got this."

"Yes, we do." Nikki took a deep breath, then let the door fall closed behind her.

"I told you I need the alarm fixed, now!" Jayden's voice boomed through the shop.

Just then Nikki recognized his voice. She had

heard him on the phone when she had been walking the dogs before Alex was killed. He'd been arguing with someone about something to do with licensing. She remembered how his short temper was on full display.

"Yes, now." Jayden slammed down the phone. "Sorry about that. The alarm company is useless." He smiled at them as they walked toward him. His short, brown hair looked a bit disheveled.

"Hi Jayden." Nikki smiled in return as she paused in front of the counter. "I just wanted to check in with you, to see how you're holding up."

"I've told you before you can't have that dog in here." Jayden looked straight at Sonia.

"Oh, don't worry, she won't cause any trouble." Sonia offered a sweet smile.

"You see that she doesn't." Jayden narrowed his eyes. "I don't want to find any fur anywhere. Or anything broken."

"She's such a doll, I promise." Sonia shifted the dog in her arms. As she did, Princess began to squirm and struggle to get to the floor.

"Jayden, can you tell me more about what happened the day Alex was murdered." Nikki locked eyes with him. "You didn't see a couple hanging around by any chance, you didn't talk to them?"

"I don't know what you're talking about." Jayden looked back at her.

Sonia opened her arms enough to invite Princess to jump down from them.

When the dog landed on the floor of the shop, she gasped.

"Princess, get back here!"

"You can't let that dog run loose in here!" Jayden crossed his arms as he glared at her. "She'll break something!"

"Don't worry, I'll get her." Sonia waved her hand as she chased after Princess.

"I'd just really like to know if anyone came in here asking questions about Alex. Or if you saw him in Woof Way with anyone else." Nikki's voice followed after Sonia as she stepped behind the counter to hunt down Princess. Each time Princess ran toward Sonia, Sonia shooed her off in a new direction. As she followed her around pretending to try to catch her, she took in the sight of everything she passed. An extra cash box stashed underneath the register. A baseball bat propped up near the door that led to the back. A stack of magazines about antiques. Nothing that screamed evidence in a murder.

Sonia shooed Princess into the back room and followed after her.

Princess ran around, then headed for a rolling shelf in the corner that contained several small, antique-looking, wooden statues.

"No Princess, don't!" Sonia lunged for the dog before she could launch herself up to the bottom layer of shelves. She swept Princess up into her arms, but her shoulder collided with the shelf, and knocked it a few feet in the opposite direction. As the shelf rolled, Sonia reached out to try to stop it. Before she could grab it, it rolled out of her reach. She caught sight of a small chute on the wall. It reminded her of a trash chute found in an apartment building, or a laundry chute. She hadn't expected to find the trash chute in the antique store. Sonia reached out and pulled it open. The hatch gave a soft squeak, but otherwise moved easily.

"Did you get that dog, yet?" Jayden barked from outside the door that led to the back.

"Just a second! I'll be right out!" Sonia snapped a picture of the chute with her phone, then carefully eased the shelves back into place.

With Princess still clutched in her arms, she

started toward the door to the back room just as Jayden swung it open.

"That beast better not have touched anything! She better not have broken anything! This stuff is expensive!"

"I know, she didn't touch anything. I'm so sorry about this. I promise I will keep Princess out of your store from now on." As Sonia stepped out of the back and into the main area of the store, she caught Nikki's eye. "Time for us to go, I think."

"Okay." Nikki held her gaze for a moment, then nodded. Nikki could tell that Sonia was eager to get out of there. "Thanks for your time, Jayden." She looked back at him. "Again, I'm sorry for the loss of your friend."

"Thanks." Jayden narrowed his eyes as he watched the two of them walk toward the door.

As soon as they were outside, Sonia grabbed Nikki by the arm and pulled her toward the alley.

"What?" Nikki followed her down the alley.

"I found this in the back of the shop." Sonia displayed the picture of the chute on her phone. "It must lead out to the dumpster, right?"

"I would guess so." Nikki nodded as she studied the picture. "But what does this have to do with anything?"

"Nothing probably." Sonia pointed down the alley. "But he had shelving in front of it, like he was trying to hide it. And it's access to the alley that we didn't know about."

"It is." Nikki surveyed the alley. "But it's just a trash chute. It doesn't mean that he had anything to do with Alex's murder. It's not like someone could fit in it to access the alley."

"No, but I still feel like it might have something to do with the murder." Sonia shook her head. "I can't explain it exactly. I just want to see where it leads."

"Jayden claimed not to know anything about any couple. He said he wasn't with Alex when the murder happened because he was on the phone for a while with the alarm company. Apparently, he's been trying to get it fixed for a while. He seemed regretful, upset that he wasn't in the alley to help Alex," Nikki explained.

"But he could have been lying."

"Of course." Nikki nodded. "Do you really think Jayden was involved?"

"I don't know, I think maybe he's holding something back. Maybe he's involved, or someone connected to him is." Sonia looked above the dumpster. "There it is." She pointed to a trash chute.

"I never really noticed it before. I wonder if it's even still used." Nikki tipped her head to the side to get a better look. "It looks really rusty."

"The dumpster does seem to be positioned so that the chute can connect with it." Sonia sighed. "I'm sorry, Nikki, I had hoped it would lead to something, but it doesn't look like it does."

"That's okay, it's good to know either way. It might lead to something else, eventually." Nikki looked toward the café. "Alex came out here. It was one of the last things that he did. He was just following his usual routine. He couldn't have known that it would be the last moments of his life."

"Do you think he suspected anything at all?" Sonia crossed her arms. "Do you think he knew that someone was after him?"

"My guess is that he felt that way all of the time. After spending time in jail, and turning so many people in, he was probably always looking over his shoulder." Nikki sighed as she walked over to the door that led from the café into the alley. "Gina had no idea what she was getting into when she hired him. This has really upset her."

"I imagine it will be even harder for her to handle if it does turn out that Mario had something to do with Alex's death." Sonia pursed her lips as she surveyed the alley again. "You know, this alley isn't very exposed. With all of the overgrowth behind it, the backs of the houses facing it, the empty apartments, the only other place for a witness to see anything was from the street side." She turned to face the side of the alley that opened onto the street. "You really don't remember anyone walking past you and Gina while you talked?"

"No one." Nikki shook her head. "I didn't even know anything was wrong until Princess started growling. I thought she had seen an animal or something. Then I heard Gina scream."

"With no witnesses, we're really stuck here." Sonia shook her head. "I hope we get some kind of lead."

"I hope so, too. I'll check in with you and Princess later, okay?"

"Sure." Sonia met her eyes. "But do be careful, Nikki. Something about this murder really has me on edge. I feel like everyone is lying to us."

"It does seem as if a lot of people have something to hide." Nikki bent down and gave Princess a kiss on the head goodbye. "Don't worry, I'll be careful."

"You don't want to get on the wrong side of a killer, especially living alone. Who knows what they might do to keep you quiet." Sonia scooped Princess up into her arms.

"You live alone, too, Sonia." Nikki crossed her arms.

"Alone?" Sonia laughed, then planted a kiss on the top of Princess' head. "Not at all. I have my trusty watchdog."

"That's true." Nikki smiled.

"I'll give you a lift." Sonia offered as they walked toward the end of the alley.

"Thanks, but I'll walk. I'm close to home." Nikki gave Princess a pet, then turned down the street. "I'll catch up with you later."

Sonia watched her go. The truth was that she loved living with Princess, but she wished her husband was still around. She missed his company. But since he had passed away she'd come to enjoy living alone over the years. Although there were times when she felt a little vulnerable because of it, the majority of the time it gave her a sense of freedom that she preferred to hold onto. But Nikki, in her twenties, still had her entire life ahead of her. She certainly couldn't spend it alone. She had found someone she loved. It filled Sonia with excitement for what the future held for Nikki.

"Let's go, Princess." Sonia started toward her

car. As she did she caught sight of someone just slipping through the door of the café. Although she saw him for only a second, she recognized him as Gina's boyfriend, Mario. She frowned as she continued down the sidewalk to her car. Could he really have been jealous enough to kill?

CHAPTER 19

Nikki pushed open the door to the bar that Mario said Alex and Jayden often went to together and stepped inside. She didn't tell Sonia she planned to go there as she had only decided to on her way home and she didn't want to worry her.

It had been a long time since Nikki had gone to that bar. Briefly, after she turned twenty-one, she went to the bar a few times with friends. But the bar had mainly been made up of older locals who were more interested in unwinding from a long day than communicating with people they considered to be children. There were a few less than genuine guys that she'd run into, but they hadn't held her interest.

Since getting involved with Quinn, she had only

been there a couple of times with him, since neither of them drank much, and both usually preferred to spend what time they had together, at home with Spots. However, she still recognized the bartender as he nodded to her from behind the bar.

"Nikki." He smiled as she walked up to him. "What brings you here? I know it's not my wit and charm." He pushed his dark blond hair back from his eyes. "Or is it? Did the local lawman finally set you free?"

"I hope not, Pete." Nikki winced as she sat down at the bar.

"It would certainly be good for the rest of us." Pete grabbed a glass and set it on the counter. "Care for something?"

"You're too kind." Nikki rolled her eyes. "I don't remember you having an ounce of interest in me. No thanks, I'm actually here for some information."

"Why does that not surprise me?" Pete put the glass back on the shelf. "The only reason I didn't go after you, Nikki, is because as everyone knows you are way too curious. Always asking questions. I knew I wouldn't meet up to your standards."

"Oh?" Nikki smiled as she met his eyes. "Do you have any dark secrets that you want to confess?"

"Taking confessions is usually my job." Pete

grinned, the edges of his eyes crinkled, and a faint laugh escaped his lips.

"Have you taken any lately?" Nikki did her best to ignore the glimmer in his eyes. "Maybe from Alex?"

"Alex?" Pete tossed a towel over his shoulder and turned away from her. "I should have known that you were here about the dead guy. Breaking my heart again, I see, just when I thought you came here to see me."

"I did come here to see you." Nikki tapped her fingertips lightly on the bar. "Because I know that you know more about the people in this town than most. Including Alex."

"He came in here, that's true." Pete glanced over his shoulder and met her eyes. "He didn't tip very good."

"I imagine not. I doubt he made very much money." Nikki pulled a ten dollar bill from her wallet and set it on the bar. "It's not much, but it might make up for those low tips."

"No, it's not much." Pete snatched it up, then turned to face her. "He was in here a lot with Jayden, the guy that owns the antique store. Those two often hung out."

"Oh, I didn't realize that they hung out here

together." Nikki didn't want him to know that she was there because she had heard they were often in the bar together. She wanted to hear what he had to say about it. "What about the night before Alex was killed? Was he in here that night?" She watched his expression closely. She looked for any twitches or winces that might indicate that he was preparing to lie to her.

"Yes, he and Jayden were in here." Pete frowned as he gazed at her. "Can you keep this between us?"

"That depends on what it is." Nikki narrowed her eyes as her heartbeat quickened.

"I don't want to have to talk to the cops, least of all, your boyfriend, got it?" Pete shuddered. "People with badges, they make me nervous."

"It sounds like you might have a guilty conscience." Nikki frowned.

"Do you want the information or not?" Pete lifted an eyebrow as he leaned closer to her.

"Yes, don't worry about the cops." Nikki knew he obviously wanted to tell someone what he knew, whatever it was must be weighing on him.

"Good." Pete lowered his voice. "Those two were in here close to closing. They were just about the last people in here. I told them both it was last call, then I started cleaning up. Next thing I know, they're shouting at each other. I thought I was going to have to break them up."

"What were they fighting about?" Nikki thought back to her conversation with Jayden. He hadn't mentioned any problems between himself and Alex.

"I'm not sure exactly. Alex said something about photographs, and Jayden lost it. He started shoving Alex and screaming at him that he wouldn't get away with it." Pete cringed as he shook his head. "I was going to separate them but then Alex just took off."

"What about Jayden? Did he follow him?" Nikki asked.

"No, he didn't go after him. He drank another beer. Sat right at that table." Pete pointed to a small table by the front door. "I had to encourage him to leave when it was time."

"Did you ask him about the argument?" Nikki gazed at him hopefully.

"No, I just wanted to be done for the night, you know?" Pete shrugged. "He was between me and locking the door. So, I just escorted him out the door, then locked up. He looked a little uneasy when I put him outside, though."

"Why do you think that is?" Nikki bit into her bottom lip.

"I don't know exactly. Maybe he thought Alex would be out there waiting for him. But when I looked outside, I didn't see anyone. I wouldn't have left him alone there, if I thought he was in danger." Pete sighed, then stroked his hand back through his hair. "Maybe if I had paid more attention to what they were arguing about, I could have helped Alex. It does bother me that one of the last places he went was my bar."

"That is unsettling." Nikki nodded as she stood up from the barstool. "When you left for the night, was Jayden still out there?"

"No, he wasn't. I figured he had just walked home. A lot of people walk to and from the bar, so they don't have to bother with a cab or a bus."

Nikki clenched her jaw as she realized that it appeared as if Jayden had a big problem with Alex.

As Nikki walked away from the bar, she noticed that the antique store was closed. With no one inside, she guessed no one would catch her, if she were to take a little peek at what Jayden might be hiding. He had mentioned he was trying to get his alarm fixed when Alex was being murdered and she had overheard him trying to get it fixed, so if it was broken she wouldn't risk setting it off.

Nikki walked down the alley to the delivery door. She tried the knob, hoping he might have left it open. Instead, it was locked. She jiggled the handle, then sighed and took a step back. Next to the door was a medium-sized window. At first glance, the window filled the frame. But as she stepped closer she noticed a small gap. Her heart raced as she slid her fingers under the sash. With some force she was able to get it up far enough to climb in.

Once inside, Nikki turned the flashlight on her phone on and headed straight for his office but paused when she caught sight of the rolling shelf that Sonia had accidently pushed aside. She walked over to it and pushed it until the small chute was revealed. It was only big enough to allow small bags of trash to go through. She pulled open the chute and shined her flashlight into the dark space. She expected it to smell but it didn't. It looked very clean, as if it hadn't been used. As she cast her flashlight over it, she noticed a faint sparkle as the flashlight passed over something caught on an edge inside the chute.

Being petite had been a disadvantage for Nikki

in many ways. She rarely got picked for the team when playing sports, and people generally treated her as if she wasn't strong enough to lift a pillow. But in this moment, she could see the benefit of being able to squeeze partway into the chute. She kept the light pointed at the shiny object and reached as far down into the chute as she could. The metal edge of the chute began to dig into her ribs as she tried to stretch a little farther. A moment of panic coursed through her as she wondered what might happen if she got stuck.

Finally, Nikki's fingertips struck something caught on the side of the chute where a screw jutted out farther than it should have. The long, thin object instantly felt like a bracelet or a necklace. She fished it free of the screw and backed out of the chute. She winced as she felt the metal edge dig in one more time. She guessed that she might get some bruises from it.

The chute snapped shut as Nikki shined the light on the object in her hand. It was long enough to be a necklace and appeared to be real gold. A pendant hung from it, containing a gemstone that sparkled when she pointed the light at it. Her heart raced as she realized how expensive it looked. Of course, she was no jewelry expert. It was possible that it was just costume jewelry. But what was it doing in the trash chute? Even if it was worthless, it was pretty enough not to want to throw away.

A loud bang made her jump and take a sharp breath. For a split-second she froze. Was someone in the store with her?

Then Nikki snapped into action. If someone was there, she needed to move as quickly as possible. There was nowhere to hide. She shoved the rolling shelf back into place, then ran for the window. It had slammed shut. Relief washed over her. That must have been the sound she'd heard. She decided to take the door instead. Once outside, she ran as fast as she could to her apartment. Exhausted and out of breath she stumbled into her kitchen for a glass of water.

"You scared yourself nearly to death, Nikki." She rolled her eyes as she took a gulp of water.

Nikki froze in the middle of the kitchen and listened closely. That thump was probably just her imagination. A bit of wind outside. Something might have toppled over. She took a deep breath, then turned on the faucet and began washing the dishes.

Another thump caused her to jump, and the glass she held slipped from her hand. It shattered against the sink in the same moment that she turned toward the front door. As she watched, the knob began to turn. She'd locked it, hadn't she? She was usually very careful about things like that. Especially now, after Alex's murder. But as the knob twisted, she couldn't be certain that she'd locked it. Only one person had a key to her front door. That was Quinn.

It must be Quinn. But if he had a key, why was it taking him so long to unlock the door? She rummaged in her purse for her phone. Where had she left it? Had it dropped out of her purse when she ran home? Her heart began to race as she realized she had no way to call for help.

The knob stopped turning. It jiggled a little, as if someone might be trying to force it open. Then it stopped doing that as well. Seconds later, something slammed hard into the door.

Nikki gasped as the door popped open, and a man stumbled through it, right into her living room.

CHAPTER 20

"Jayden!" Nikki took a few steps back as she glared at him. "What are you doing?"

"What are you doing?" Jayden pointed at her as he took a step forward, then almost fell over.

"You're drunk." Nikki grabbed a frying pan from the stove. "You need to leave before I call the police."

"Sure, call the police." Jayden burped, then swung his arm through the air. "Call your little boyfriend. Tell him that you think I would kill my friend!"

"Stop it, Jayden!" Nikki held the pan in front of her. "Don't take a step closer. I mean it!"

"Or what?" Jayden laughed, then leaned heavily on the side of the couch. "You're going to cook me up?"

"Out, Jayden!" Nikki lowered the frying pan. A stumbling drunk didn't seem like much of a threat to her. "I know you're upset about what happened to Alex. I'm sure it wasn't your fault. Just go home and sleep it off, alright?"

"Home?" Jayden looked into her eyes. "Do you think I can make it home like this?"

"I don't care where you make it, you just have to get out of here!" Nikki gave him a light shove toward the door.

The moment Nikki touched him, his arms snapped around her and squeezed so hard that she could barely breathe. She looked into his eyes and found them to be clear and sharp. He closed his hand over her mouth before she had the chance to scream.

"You aren't as clever as you think, are you?" Jayden smirked as he pressed his palm harder against her mouth. "Fell for the drunk and helpless trick, didn't you?" He wrestled her toward the door. "Nikki, if you fight me, I can make this a lot worse."

Nikki's chest tightened as thoughts of how he

could make it worse flooded her mind. Still, she struggled to get free of his grasp. She knew that the moment he had her alone, somewhere no one could hear her scream, he would do what he had planned to do from the beginning. He would kill her. She had to fight, she had to make a sound, to let someone know she was in trouble. If only she had her phone she might have been able to call for help.

As Jayden pulled Nikki through the door, she kicked out at it in an attempt to make as much noise as she could.

"This is your last warning." Jayden jerked her toward his waiting car. "If you continue to cause all of this trouble, it won't just be you, do you hear me? If someone lets your boyfriend know that you've been taken, what do you think he's going to do?" He tightened his arms around her as she bucked against him. "That's right. He'll come looking for you. When he does, I'll have to kill him, too. Is that what you really want?"

Tears slid down Nikki's cheeks at the thought. She relaxed enough to allow him to push her into the back seat of the car. As the door slammed closed behind her, a scream stuck in her throat. Quinn would come for her. He would do absolutely anything to save her. She would do anything to protect him, too.

"Jayden, you shouldn't do this." Nikki spoke as calmly as she could as he started the car. "You're only going to make things worse for yourself."

"Am I?" Jayden glanced in the rearview mirror. "I know that you were sneaking around in my shop tonight. I saw you run out of there. I checked the camera, and I saw you halfway inside the trash chute." He drove in the direction of the antique store. "I'm guessing, Nikki, that you already know too much. Don't you?"

Nikki's heart raced as she began to put a few things together in her mind. Jayden obviously didn't want her looking in the trash chute. Maybe the trash chute was hidden, because it wasn't used for trash. Maybe that's why the necklace had been inside. But what could it have been used for?

"Jayden, what did you do?"

"You know, when I met Alex, I thought we would be great friends. With his criminal history, I was sure he'd be able to help with my side business. So, I told him about it, and invited him to be part of it. Since our only pawn shop owner in town is such a by-the-book kind of guy, I knew there was a hole to fill. I could fill it. People need to be able to sell stolen goods. So, I offered a service to them. I explained how I got the merchandise in and out of the shop to Alex, thinking he'd love to help."

"The trash chute." Nikki's eyes widened.

"Yes, people would drop off stolen goods as if they were selling me legitimate things that were theirs. Then all I had to do was get my delivery driver to notify me he was on the way to the alley and I would get the stolen stuff into the dumpster, then the delivery driver would snag it before the trash was picked up. He takes it far enough out of town and sells it to a fence. It's a perfect system really. Until Alex disappointed me." Jayden pulled into the parking lot of the antique store.

"He wanted nothing to do with it?" Nikki grimaced.

"I thought he would be happy to join in. He had lots of contacts. But when I told him that my business was growing and the first step was to get the café shut down, so that I could own the businesses on both sides of the alley and avoid suspicious eyes, I guess he didn't like it. He was going to warn Gina that I'd been calling in complaints about the café to the licensing board to get it shut down. He even called the board to try and find out exactly what I had told them. Then he took pictures of my delivery driver picking up the stolen goods, and of the trash chute in my shop." Jayden frowned.

"He was going to turn you in?" Nikki wanted to keep him talking.

"Yes. He told me that if I continued to mess with Gina's business, he would turn me in to the police." Jayden rolled his eyes. "Can you believe it?" He chuckled. "Here I thought I could trust a hardened criminal, but I guess not. I had to get rid of him. The plan was for me to kill Alex, and my driver to pick up his body before anyone noticed. The killing part was easy enough. I made up an alibi, then just slipped through the back door and around the corner of my shop."

"You were in the alley the whole time?" Nikki prompted.

"I was. I hid beside the dumpster and waited for Alex to toss in the trash. The moment he opened the dumpster, I shot him. He didn't even have time to scream. It would have worked, too, if it weren't for Gina." Jayden scowled. "She just had to muck things up by finding the body before my guy could pick it up." He sighed as he turned the car off. "I wish it was her in my back seat. I'd enjoy killing her much more. But it's you." He turned to face her.

Nikki opened her mouth to scream, but before she could he grabbed the baseball bat from the floorboard of the passenger seat and swung it hard against her head.

CHAPTER 21

The moment she'd heard the sirens, Sonia's pulse went into overdrive. She'd been calling Nikki for over an hour with no response. She'd even called Quinn to go check on her at her apartment. But Sonia had no response from either. Those sirens drove her right out the door and into her car. With Princess perched in her lap, she drove toward the sound of the sirens.

"Please Nikki, be okay." Sonia clutched the steering wheel tightly. Though she'd never had children of her own, since she'd become so close to Nikki, she finally understood what it was like to worry about someone that you cared for so deeply. Nikki wasn't her daughter, but she was her closest friend, and she would do anything to protect her.

Sonia made it to the center of town before she smelled the smoke. Her stomach twisted with fear as she spotted the large firetrucks parked in front of the café and antique store. Her mind jumped from possibility to possibility as she saw the flames jumping through the front windows of the antique store.

Sonia parked in the middle of the street and launched herself out of the car. Princess stuck to her heels as she searched the crowd for a familiar face.

"Mrs. Whitter!" Quinn ran over to her.

"Is she in there? Please don't tell me she's in there!" Sonia gasped, then coughed on the smoke that filled the air.

"Mrs. Whitter, she wasn't at her apartment, and it looked like someone had forced their way in. There was a broken glass." Quinn's eyes widened as he stumbled over his words. "We don't know where she is, but she's not inside the antique store."

"We have to get in there!" Sonia grabbed Quinn's arm and gave it a hard tug. "Quinn! She's in there! I know she is!"

"The firemen have been through the whole shop." Quinn put his hands on her shoulders and looked into her eyes. "She's not in there, Sonia. I know you're frightened, I am, too, but she's not in there!"

"You don't understand!" Sonia ripped away from his grasp and shrieked her words. "I haven't been able to reach her. There's only one reason she wouldn't answer her phone. She's in there, Quinn!" Her heart raced as she felt certain that her friend was in danger. She picked up Princess and ran straight down the alley. She noticed that the delivery door of the antique store was open a bit.

"Sonia, don't!" Quinn's heavy footsteps pounded after her. "Stop! It's not safe!"

"Please, I have to get in there." Sonia's voice trembled as tears flooded her eyes.

"Sonia!" Quinn wrapped his arms around her and Princess and held tight. "Stop! You're going to get yourself killed, and Nikki will never forgive either of us for that." He looked into her eyes. "You can't go in there. You have to stay out here. It's too dangerous."

"I need to go inside." As Sonia's body shuddered with the force of her fear, Princess jumped out of her arms and landed on the ground.

"Princess!" Sonia gasped. "Get back here!"

Princess barked and ran straight toward the delivery door. Sonia ran after her.

"No, Princess, don't!"

"Sonia! What are you doing? Stop!" Quinn turned to run after her.

"Princess!" Sonia lunged in an attempt to grab Princess before she could disappear through the gap in the delivery door, but she couldn't catch her. She could hear the dog barking wildly. She tried to push the delivery door open but it wouldn't move. Something was pressed against it and stopped it from opening farther. "Quinn!" She gasped as she turned to face him. "I have to get to her!"

Quinn grabbed her by the arms. "I'm sorry about this, Mrs. Whitter. I really am." He looked into her eyes as he snapped handcuffs on her. "I can't let you go in there."

"Quinn! I know that Nikki is in there, and now Princess is, too!" Tears spilled down Sonia's cheeks. She prided herself on barely ever crying, but in that moment she felt as if every tear she had ever held back burst forth.

"She'll come back out, Mrs. Whitter. When she smells the smoke, she'll get scared and come back out." Quinn led her to a nearby patrol car and opened the door. "Watch her." He looked at the officer. "Don't let her out of your sight."

"Yes, sir." The officer nodded, though he looked

at Sonia strangely. "Are the handcuffs necessary, sir?"

"Yes, trust me." Quinn frowned as he looked into Sonia's eyes again. "I just want to make sure you're safe, Mrs. Whitter."

"What about Nikki?" Sonia's voice broke as she spoke. "Who's making sure she's safe? What about Princess?"

Quinn straightened up and looked toward the antique store. He gazed at it for just a moment, then jogged back down into the alley. Seconds later, he ran back out and straight for the front door of the antique store.

"Someone's inside!" Quinn shouted at the firemen. "I can hear her calling for help! It's Nikki! She's inside!"

"Quinn!" Sonia jumped to her feet, but the officer stopped her from getting any farther.

"I'm sorry, ma'am, but you have to stay here." The officer frowned.

"Like you can keep me here!" Sonia growled and kicked him hard in the shin.

"Ouch!" The officer placed her into the car. He closed the door, and she heard the locks engage.

Sonia peered through the window as she realized there was no escape. She could only hope that the firemen would get to Nikki in time. As she watched, Quinn ran in right after the firemen.

Seconds later, a fireman emerged, with his jacket bundled up in his arms. Behind him, Quinn stepped out, with Nikki draped across his shoulder. He ran straight for the ambulance, as the fireman headed for the patrol car.

"Please, let me out!" Sonia pounded on the window, relieved that Quinn had been kind enough to handcuff her hands in the front.

"Open it up." The fireman instructed the officer.

"Are you sure?" The officer frowned. "She's a little crazy."

"I'm sure." The fireman nodded.

The officer opened the door and remained out of Sonia's kicking range.

"Ma'am." The fireman crouched down in front of her. "Your dog saved that young woman's life." He began to unfold his jacket. "We checked for anyone inside, but we didn't find anyone, no one answered our calls. She was hidden behind some shelving in the storage room and must have been unconscious. My guess is that this little pup managed to wake her up. Then Detective Grant was able to hear her calls for help through the trash chute in the alley." He pulled back the final flap of his jacket to reveal Princess curled up in the folds of the large garment. "If it wasn't for your pup, I don't think we ever would have found her."

"Princess!" Sonia gasped as she looked at the still dog in the fireman's arms. "Oh, my precious baby." She stroked her head and kissed her cheeks.

Princess' eyes fluttered open. She looked into Sonia's eyes, then gave a quiet bark.

"She's okay." The fireman stroked the dog's fur. "She's just a little stunned, I think."

"My love!" Sonia scooped Princess into her arms and held her close. "What about Nikki?" She looked into the fireman's eyes. "Is she going to be okay?"

CHAPTER 22

Bright light, and a terrible smell, made it impossible for Nikki to feel good about waking up. She winced as she touched the bandage on her forehead. As the hospital room came into focus, she heard Quinn's voice.

"It's okay, sweetheart, you're safe. You're going to be just fine." Quinn squeezed her hand. "We have Jayden in custody. He's admitted to everything. But I want you to tell me what happened, Nikki." He stroked her cheek.

"I found a necklace in the trash chute in Jayden's shop." Nikki reached for her pocket, but found she was in a hospital gown. "He saw me looking in the chute. He broke into my apartment and kidnapped me. He hit me. That's the last thing I remember." She sighed. "He hit me with the bat, and then I woke up to Princess licking my cheeks. I don't even remember him putting me in the store or starting the fire."

"It's okay." Quinn stroked the back of her hand with his thumb as he perched on the chair beside her hospital bed. "He's given us a full confession. He saw you in the store, he thought that you knew too much. He thought you had worked out he was dealing in stolen goods and had killed Alex."

"Well, I didn't know what was happening, but when I saw the chute I was suspicious." Nikki nodded. "He admitted to me what he was doing with the chute when he took me. It was a clever way to avoid anyone seeing what was happening."

"It was. The delivery guy has a criminal record, so if someone saw him going in and out of the shop all the time it could have brought a lot of unwanted attention on Jayden. The Hales, the couple that was after Alex, came to Jayden, hoping that Alex had tried to sell him the jewelry. But he hadn't." Quinn held up his phone to show Nikki a recent picture of them. "They really are masters of disguise."

"Wow." Nikki's eyes widened. "They were the couple snooping around Gina's house. They said they were her neighbors. They looked so different in the other photos the FBI showed me. I had no idea. I didn't recognize them before."

"The Hales saw Alex go in the shed in Woof Way a few times and they stole the key to search the shed, but they didn't find the jewelry there. Jayden suspected Alex had the jewelry and he also thought maybe he had hidden it in the shed. So, after Jayden killed Alex he took Gina's keys to the shed from him. When the police had left the scene he managed to find the jewelry there because he often saw Alex go to a toolbox in the shed. The jewelry was hidden at the bottom of it in a secret compartment. The Hales didn't manage to find it but he did."

"I presume he went into the store after he murdered Alex." Nikki frowned. "Why was the murder weapon in the bushes, if he didn't run away?"

"He wiped it down and threw it there in case his store was searched." Quinn shook his head. "He's a very calculating man. When he realized it was going to be harder than he thought to take over Gina's café, he decided he wanted to set up his business elsewhere. He tried to burn down the store. There was nothing really valuable in it. He would get the insurance from it and get rid of—" Quinn's voice broke as he squeezed her hand again. "I can't even imagine what you went through, Nikki. I'm so sorry I wasn't there to protect you."

"Don't be." Nikki looked into his eyes with a small smile. "You did save me. You, and Sonia, and Princess."

"Yes, and Princess." Quinn nodded. "I am going to buy that dog so many treats. I'm so relieved everything turned out okay."

"Me, too." Nikki never thought she would be lucky enough to end up with Quinn. The boy she had a crush on all those years ago. "How did I come across someone as wonderful as you?" She looked into his eyes and smiled.

"You faked drowning a couple of times." Quinn shrugged, then grinned.

"Funny." Nikki laughed.

"I have decided that I want to make sure we spend more time together." Quinn squeezed her hand. "Starting with now. You are being discharged. I am going to take you home and take care of you."

"That sounds great to me. I can't wait to spend time with my favorite companion." Nikki slowly sat up in the bed.

"Me, too." Quinn's eyes brightened. "I can't wait to spend time with you."

"Oh, I meant spending time with Spots, but I guess you could come along, too, if it's okay with him." Nikki shrugged.

"Oh, look who's feeling all better." Quinn hugged her. "I love you, Nikki."

"I love you too, Quinn." Nikki kissed him. "Always."

The End

ABOUT THE AUTHOR

Cindy Bell is a USA Today and Wall Street Journal Bestselling Author. She is the author of the Little Leaf Creek, Wagging Tail, Donut Truck, Dune House, Sage Gardens, Chocolate Centered, Macaron Patisserie, Nuts about Nuts, Bekki the Beautician, Heavenly Highland Inn and Wendy the Wedding Planner cozy mystery series.

Cindy has always loved reading, but it is only recently that she has discovered her passion for writing romantic cozy mysteries. She loves walking along the beach thinking of the next adventure her characters can embark on.

You can sign up for her newsletter so you are notified of her latest releases at http://www.cindybellbooks.com.

ALSO BY CINDY BELL

WAGGING TAIL COZY MYSTERIES

Murder at Pawprint Creek (prequel)

Murder at Pooch Park

Murder at the Pet Boutique

A Merry Murder at St. Bernard Cabins

Murder at the Dog Training Academy

Murder at Corgi Country Club

A Merry Murder on Ruff Road

Murder at Poodle Place

Murder at Hound Hill

Murder at Rover Meadows

Murder at the Pet Expo

Murder on Woof Way

DUNE HOUSE COZY MYSTERIES

Seaside Secrets

Boats and Bad Guys

Treasured History

[Hidden Hideaways](#)

[Dodgy Dealings](#)

[Suspects and Surprises](#)

[Ruffled Feathers](#)

[A Fishy Discovery](#)

[Danger in the Depths](#)

[Celebrities and Chaos](#)

[Pups, Pilots and Peril](#)

[Tides, Trails and Trouble](#)

[Racing and Robberies](#)

[Athletes and Alibis](#)

[Manuscripts and Deadly Motives](#)

[Pelicans, Pier and Poison](#)

[Sand, Sea and a Skeleton](#)

[Pianos and Prison](#)

[Relaxation, Reunions and Revenge](#)

[A Tangled Murder](#)

[Fame, Food and Murder](#)

[Beaches and Betrayal](#)

LITTLE LEAF CREEK COZY MYSTERY SERIES

Chaos in Little Leaf Creek

Peril in Little Leaf Creek

Conflict in Little Leaf Creek

Action in Little Leaf Creek

Vengeance in Little Leaf Creek

Greed in Little Leaf Creek

Surprises in Little Leaf Creek

Missing in Little Leaf Creek

Haunted in Little Leaf Creek

Trouble in Little Leaf Creek

CHOCOLATE CENTERED COZY MYSTERIES

The Sweet Smell of Murder

A Deadly Delicious Delivery

A Bitter Sweet Murder

A Treacherous Tasty Trail

Pastry and Peril

Trouble and Treats

Fudge Films and Felonies

Custom-Made Murder

Skydiving, Soufflés and Sabotage

Christmas Chocolates and Crimes

Hot Chocolate and Homicide

Chocolate Caramels and Conmen

Picnics, Pies and Lies

Devils Food Cake and Drama

Cinnamon and a Corpse

Cherries, Berries and a Body

Christmas Cookies and Criminals

Grapes, Ganache & Guilt

Yule Logs & Murder

Mocha, Marriage and Murder

SAGE GARDENS COZY MYSTERIES

Sage Gardens Cozy Mystery Series Box Set Volume 1 (Books 1 - 4)

Birthdays Can Be Deadly

Money Can Be Deadly

Trust Can Be Deadly

Ties Can Be Deadly

Rocks Can Be Deadly

Jewelry Can Be Deadly

Numbers Can Be Deadly

Memories Can Be Deadly

Paintings Can Be Deadly

Snow Can Be Deadly

Tea Can Be Deadly

Greed Can Be Deadly

Clutter Can Be Deadly

NUTS ABOUT NUTS COZY MYSTERIES

A Tough Case to Crack

A Seed of Doubt

Roasted Peanuts and Peril

Chestnuts, Camping and Culprits

DONUT TRUCK COZY MYSTERIES

Deadly Deals and Donuts

Fatal Festive Donuts

Bunny Donuts and a Body

Strawberry Donuts and Scandal

Frosted Donuts and Fatal Falls

BEKKI THE BEAUTICIAN COZY MYSTERIES

Hairspray and Homicide

A Dyed Blonde and a Dead Body

Mascara and Murder

Pageant and Poison

Conditioner and a Corpse

Mistletoe, Makeup and Murder

Hairpin, Hair Dryer and Homicide

Blush, a Bride and a Body

Shampoo and a Stiff

Cosmetics, a Cruise and a Killer

Lipstick, a Long Iron and Lifeless

Camping, Concealer and Criminals

Treated and Dyed

A Wrinkle-Free Murder

A MACARON PATISSERIE COZY MYSTERY SERIES

Sifting for Suspects

Recipes and Revenge

Mansions, Macarons and Murder

HEAVENLY HIGHLAND INN COZY MYSTERIES

Murdering the Roses

Dead in the Daisies

Killing the Carnations

Drowning the Daffodils

Suffocating the Sunflowers

Books, Bullets and Blooms

A Deadly Serious Gardening Contest

A Bridal Bouquet and a Body

Digging for Dirt

WENDY THE WEDDING PLANNER COZY MYSTERIES

Matrimony, Money and Murder

Chefs, Ceremonies and Crimes

Knives and Nuptials

Mice, Marriage and Murder